I0771833

Epigraph

The universe is unfair and different for every creature. We all eat, sleep, and live, but we experience it in different ways. For some, it is painful, for others, full of laughter and love. Our world is formed by the perception of those who live in it.

When we leave the mortal realm, it is only then that we are truly judged. One and all, returned to the void of creation for the place where karma truly exists.

In death, may you all find satisfaction. May you all find solace. May you all find peace...

In death, again and again, may you find the universe bigger than you ever perceived...

Tahn Riven, Eulogy of the Collapse

Contents

Prologue

Utah Territory, 1847

Whack! The man sank to his knees as the empty spittoon fell to the floor with a dull clang. Wheezing, Domino kneeled over the body and felt for breath, making sure he hadn't killed the idiot. He was thankful to find him still alive.

He glanced up to see how his friends were doing and groaned when he realized that he still had more fighting to do. Rather than pick up his previous weapon, Domino leaned over the bar and grabbed a bottle. He was sorry to see it was still mostly full of whiskey when he launched it at his next target of choice.

The bottle collided with a skinny man, who looked barely big enough to keep from blowing away in the wind that often blew through this part of the Americas. Domino watched as the cheap bottle broke on contact with the man's skull and the man went crashing to the floor, freeing up his friend to make the last fight three-on-one.

As one, the three fell on the last of their aggressors, picking the man up and tossing him bodily out the wooden doors that swung to allow easy access and egress to the drinking establishment and hotel. They stood, looking at the man who decided not to come back for more, before going back inside to clean up.

"Damnable cowards, fight fair instead of like the spic and the limey with ya!" the man said, as he scurried away.

Ignoring the man, the three quickly went back inside, picked up the two unconscious men, tossing them out into the street as well. It said a lot about how the three were treated, as they were accustomed to such fights. They'd never once sat down for a drink peacefully in a new town.

Their current drinking establishment was nicer than many of the ones they visited. The bartender *actually* served them and decided stepping back was easier when the fighting started. He'd even given them a room for a fair price that night, which was much needed. It had been a couple of weeks since they'd slept in actual beds. Domino sat on one of the six still-standing stools and grabbed a fresh drink, taking in the whiskey.

"You paying for the damages?" The bartender asked.

"Yeah, at least for the whiskey we wasted." Domino answered, placing a dollar on the bar. "How much is a room for the night? Three beds. We can wait to have one brought over if needed."

The bartender sniffed before answering, "Two dollars. Up front. Gets you breakfast in the morning and one beer with it."

Domino nodded to the man, passing over another couple of dollars and receiving a room key for the trouble. It had the number three emblazoned on it.

"Watashitachi no heya ni ikimasu?" he asked the man behind him, previously described as a 'spic.'

"What'd you say to him?" The bartender demanded quickly, as the designated man took the key and made his way up.

"I just told him to head upstairs is all. We don't need more trouble than we've already had."

"I'll head up too," said the other party, called Limey by the cowardly man.

The bartender nodded at the man before saying, "Door's got a deadbolt on it."

"Thanks, mate," he said, taking himself upstairs with the first man.

When the first two went upstairs, it left the cowboy alone at the bar with the bartender, who looked at him.

"I know there's a story, and part of me wants it, but I'll hold off. I'm sure you've told it more than a few times." Domino laughed shortly, telling the bartender he was spot on, before taking a quarter out of a pocket and placing it on the counter.

"I'm looking for 'Big' Tim Stickland and the boys he runs with." Domino said just after he finished his laugh in a low voice. The bartender's eyes rose a little at the mention of the name, and his hand hesitated as it lowered over the quarter.

"That name ain't good to bandy about, son. What business you got with the family?"

"There's a little family just over the Nevada border that doesn't have a home anymore. There's a little girl a days' ride from there that no longer has a father." Both men knew there was more to say, but Domino stopped there.

With a sigh of resignation, the bartender slipped the quarter into his pocket and shook his head slowly.

"Fine. You paid for it. I'll have what you want by the morning. Do me a favor and leave your measurements here just in case." Domino didn't need to be told they were for his casket, should he be unlucky.

Changing the subject, Domino cast his eyes over the bar. He saw a few patrons had come in since the fight and were settling into their routines of gambling and drinking. In the corner, near a stage fit for a single person, sat a piano.

"Anyone play those keys for you?" He asked the bartender.

"Not since the last one asked the same question you did. Never saw him after that day." The bartender shook his head sadly at the statement, recalling the man.

"Mind if I play?"

Part 1: Shawn Wraine

All Wraine Comes to an End

Axis of Anarchy Publishing and Design

Chapter 1

S hawn sat at the desk, the hyperventilation finally stopping enough for him to gather his thoughts. The doctor across from him sat in silence, having given him the words he hadn't seen coming from a mile away. He looked from point to point in the office, his vision zooming in on different objects, looking for something, anything, to help him focus.

Shawn knew things had been getting tougher for him lately. At his job working construction, lifting bags of cement had been getting tougher lately. He'd been losing his breath easier, and his appetite wasn't what it used to be. He noticed that he'd been losing weight since he'd had to buy a new belt just to keep his jeans above his legs.

His son had browbeaten him mercilessly to see a doctor, and loving his son the way he did, he'd finally given in just to give the boy some peace of mind. He'd been prepared for the doctor to tell him he had some kind of bug that was going around, but he hadn't been prepared for the absolute bombshell that had been dropped on his reality.

He had so much more he wanted to do, so many things he wanted to see. He knew finding love again wasn't something he cared for, but he wanted to see his son fall in love, once, for real, at least. He wanted to watch his son bring the world that he'd created to life for millions of people more. He wanted to finish all the stories that he'd started... so many stories he wanted to finish.

Breathe in, breathe out, breathe in, breathe out, Shawn repeated the words to himself like a mantra while the doctor watched him with a clinical detachment that would have made his son jealous. The doctor's eyes softened a little, looking at Shawn, and he lost the quality of detachment.

"I've never had to tell that to anyone, Shawn." The doctor, his friend of nearly twenty years, said. "I've never wanted to have to say it." Shawn looked closely at the doctor, using his pained face to focus on something outside of his reeling mind. What he saw there was genuine, and it almost made it worse. He watched him take his glasses off and pinch the bridge of his nose before speaking again, "Do you want to tell Caellum, or should I? It might be easier coming from me."

Thinking of telling his son made him feel a little sick inside, not because he didn't want his son to know, but the thought of bringing it up made him feel ill again, like once he told his son, there wasn't any taking it back. This was the third time he'd come to the office in the last few weeks, and there had been tests the first two times. This time was all talk... just like the one he needed to have with his son.

"No. I need to be the one to tell him. He needs to hear it from me. Thanks, Wayne." The doctor nodded at Shawn.

"Take some time and let it sink in, Shawn. There are a lot of treatment options out there, but at your stage of cancer, I honestly don't know if any will be effective long term. At this point, you could be gone in ten months, or you could be gone in two years. I don't know which one, but it will happen... probably sooner rather than later."

Shawn nodded at the doctor and rose from his chair. "I'll be in touch. Thanks for being honest with me." Shawn paused as he stood before the entrance to the doctor's office and asked the question he already knew the answer to. "Is there any chance you're wrong about my chances here?"

Wayne looked at him, having seen the question coming before Shawn had voiced it. "No. When I had my suspicions, we took extra pictures to make sure. That's why I had you come in a second-time last week. After what I saw the first time, I wanted to be sure before I told you." Shawn looked at Wayne and saw the defeated look on his friend's face and knew there wasn't any more to say.

He finished opening the door and walked out of the office. He didn't remember much about the walk out of the building. He vaguely recalled the receptionist wishing him a good afternoon and his dead-pan response for her to have one as well.

He got to his car, a beat-up old blue Pontiac, and sat down in the driver's seat. He didn't quite know what to do except sit there. He pulled out his phone and thought about calling his boss to let him know he'd be back to work soon, but felt his arm go limp at the thought of talking to another human.

He looked down at the blank screen of his phone, sitting near the emergency brake on the center console, just behind the shifter, and noticed the picture he had sitting there. It was an old picture, taken once upon a time when he and his son had still lived in Minnesota. He was at a hockey game and he and his son had on matching jerseys.

There was a bright light just behind the two of them in the stands as they took the poor selfie. It was his favorite picture of the two of them... He hadn't seen a hockey game live since that time, nearly twenty years past. It was the just before they'd had to leave because of some complications beyond their control.

Now they lived in California, but it wasn't quite the same, even disregarding the politics. He missed the pace of life he'd had. He missed the stories he'd gotten to share with his son without having to worry so much about making enough money to make ends meet. He'd given his son a taste of everything he loved. In doing so, he had been able to support his son in expanding on some of those ideas. Some of which worked very well in California.

Shawn tilted his head back and closed his eyes as he flashed through thousands of moments with his son. He hadn't been a jerk or an idiot as a teenager, as many were, but had stayed close to Shawn, knowing his father had it tough doing his best to support them both.

He'd become a fantastic man by the end of it, and at twenty-eight he had advanced enough that he even owned his own home in a terrifyingly expensive part of the country. He could write his own ticket, and the only thing he had ever struggled with was having a relationship go any deeper than casual.

He'd hoped that was changing with this newest one, but the jury was still out, as far as he could tell. His thoughts spiraled back to the knowledge he needed to tell people what was happening, and once again, he opened his eyes to attempt it. He lifted the phone to his ear and felt it drop a second time.

This time, when it dropped to his side, he felt it slip from his fingers and he knew he wouldn't be talking to anyone for at least a little while. Shawn brought his hand up to cover his eyes from the sun that was spilling in through the front windshield and noticed a wetness coat the inside of his hand.

Shocked at what he felt, Shawn lowered his hand to look into his own eyes in the rearview mirror and saw twin streams dribbling down his face. He tried breathing deeply and felt his breath catch and he hiccupped slightly as he sat alone in his car, unable to do anything about the inevitable.

Shawn sat in his car for at least another hour, although he had no idea how long it had actually been. He finally stopped lamenting about what he couldn't change and had calmed down enough that he at least knew one thing he could do. He picked up his phone and looked at the screen, which he now turned on. There, he saw the picture of him and his son again. That was also the wallpaper on his phone.

He took another deep breath and looked at his face again in the mirror and saw bloodshot eyes staring back at him. He knew the first thing he'd do and dialed the number for his boss.

"Hey, it's Shawn," he said into the call when he heard the familiar voice of his boss on the other side, "Something's come up. I won't be in today. I'll tell you about it tomorrow, okay?"

"You can't tell me now, Shawn? You've never called off work before. In ten years, you've been as dependable as the sun." The voice he heard was concerned, which didn't surprise Shawn. He'd taken on the work of two people and didn't take the pay of two, although he made more than anyone else on their crew.

"I'll come in a little early tomorrow and we can have a chat about it, alright? I just need the rest of the day to deal with myself. Sorry about this." Shawn hung up the phone without waiting for a reply and laughed a little for the first time in hours. The look on his boss's face when he quit tomorrow would be *priceless*.

He kept laughing even though he knew it wasn't *that* funny. He laughed and laughed until his voice caught again and he needed to stop to breathe. *What the hell?* He thought to himself. It really wasn't funny enough to make him laugh like this, but here it was. Just one single thing to laugh at when the day was going so horribly wrong.

He remembered again the things he'd done with his son, introducing him to an entire world, a set of realities that combined to make up the cosmos, and the stories that could happen there. He thought about how his son had made a career out of telling those same stories, and making new ones.

Looking back on everything they'd shared, he had a memory come up in his mind of the first time he had done a role-playing session with his son. He remembered it had taken nearly four hours for his son to make his first character, and he'd named him something silly, *Mith,* he remembered.

They'd done the session when Caellum was still too young to be incredibly creative with his responses, but he'd been old enough to fall in love with the world of their imagination quickly. He remembered when that character had died and he had to explain to his son that he had to make a new character.

In fact, the more Shawn thought about it, he was sure he'd saved that character sheet and it was in a book or storage somewhere. He knew it'd take all day to find the thing, but with nothing else to do in his day, he decided to single-mindedly search for it, since it would take his mind off of his other pressing concerns.

He imagined that with how he felt, and along with the other things he had to take care of, it might even take a couple of days. In a slight expression of cowardice he wasn't used to, he hoped it did so he could put off the necessary conversation.

Once he found the paper, he'd tell his son. That would give him time to process his life and where he wanted to go with the time he had left. He still had to tell his son, though. He looked back to the window, and saw a small glint of steel in his eyes again, even through the redness.

Chapter 2

S hawn looked at his son with some humor. It had been a couple of weeks since Shawn had received the news of his impending death, and he had more or less come to terms with it. If he were being honest with himself, he knew he was only just hanging on to his mental state, but he'd kept busy and avoided truly dealing with it.

"Yeah, Son, there's no easy way to tell you. I'm... gonna die. I've got a few months and then I'm out; it kinda sucks, haha." He laughed a little at the mostly blank look his son was giving him. He knew the shock was taking its toll on the boy, and he knew him well enough to look into his eyes for the emotions he rarely showed anyone else.

He continued, as his son wasn't ready to contribute to the conversation yet, "Don't look at me like that, boy. Things happen." He shrugged at his son, having read him like a book, "On the upside, you should have heard my boss when I told him I quit the other day. It almost made terminal cancer worth it!"

He watched his son close his eyes and shake his head slowly, and his shoulder-length blond hair swayed from side to side with the motion. He knew some of his jokes didn't land right, and this had been one of those, clearly. He looked into his son's bright blue eyes,

"I told you first, Caellum. It's up to you to tell who you want, but I imagine I'll probably have to tell Hansen to just keep my computer."

Shawn tried, but couldn't help but add in a bitter mutter, "Not like I can take it with me.

"For now, son, I'm good. I can still do everything I've been doing." He inhaled deeply. "Just with freedom now. I've got enough time to go live in some virtual worlds and revisit my favorite stories. Beyond that, I look forward to seeing how your group destroys all of your carefully laid plans in the next few episodes of your show,"

Shawn laughed a few short bursts of air from his chest. He could hear how it wasn't as vibrant a laugh as it used to be. Even to his own ears, he sounded a little tired. He dismissed it with a quick change of subject. "Here in a little while, I may need a little help. I'll let you know."

His son nodded at him, then sat there for a few minutes, just trying to collect his thoughts. After the first minute, he could see the silence change in quality as his son took him in with a critical eye. He knew what his son saw, since he saw the same in the mirror every day now. Shawn was thinner than he had been, not quite malnourished, but his clothes were definitely looser.

His face begun to show some of that rapid weight loss as well, thinning out even more, and the few wrinkles he'd developed had become more pronounced. Once upon a time, he'd been an enormous man at just over six feet, four inches tall and weighing in at two-hundred forty-two pounds, all of it muscle. His hair was dark blond, and it had just begun to lighten. He knew when he looked in the mirror he wasn't likely to see it turn naturally gray.

Rather than dive down that particular rabbit hole again, Shawn cleared his throat and started talking again, changing the subject from his illness, "In other news, I have a new..." He paused a little and let the word draw out for a minute as if contemplating if it were the right choice. Making up his mind, he continued, "—character for you."

He was determined to keep living the best he could, as if nothing were different, at least for a little while. He was just on vacation now. He got out two simple sheets of paper from the bag he kept handy and set them to the side for his son to pick up. They were ordinary looking, but worn with time. The one on top looked like it was twenty years old if it was a day, and the boxes and numbers that sat on the page were written by both a careful and inexperienced hand, as if by a child.

Shawn watched his son while he relived again the times he'd spent teaching his son how to play tabletop roleplaying games and how his little boy had bravely battled back tears as his first character died. A couple of years later, he recalled how, even when frustrated, angry, and perhaps even a little broken, his son had stopped showing emotion.

He could feel a small growl at the back of his throat, at the memory of that family and what they had done to his son... and how he'd lacked the ability to do anything but pick up his life and try starting over with Caellum. Now that his son was grown, he'd have loved the opportunity to punch out that kid and his two lawyer parents.

Once upon a time, Shawn had gotten a call from work and told he needed to pick up his son, who was about to be expelled from school. Shawn had asked what his son had done to deserve expulsion at ten years old, and he'd been told it would be easier to come to the office and talk in person, adult to adult.

He'd gone and sat in shocked silence, then furious frustration as the principal explained to him that Caellum really had done nothing wrong, except stand up for himself. Everyone knew it. Unfortunately, the kid he'd stood up to had come from a family that the school didn't have the ability to go against.

This kid, as Shawn had never learned his name, had taken things that Caellum had been working on (he couldn't remember exactly what) and tossed them in the trash just because he could. When Caellum hadn't cooperated with his things being damaged, he'd tried to walk away.

What had ensued, had been witnessed by a teacher, when this little punk spun Caellum around and punched him in the face. Caellum had done exactly what Shawn had taught him and fought back, and fought back dirty. The fight had ended with Caellum straddling this kid's chest and using his knees to keep his arms pinned while he went to work on the punk's face.

It made Shawn more than a little proud to hear in the explanation that he'd knocked out a tooth from the kid. But honestly, what had become of it wasn't worth even the pride he'd had in his son. If it had gone wrong, and really gone wrong, he wouldn't have been able to protect his son from what would have happened.

If they handled it like they would any other similar situation, the principal had no doubt they would likely force the school to close due to lack of funding for staff. He was dead certain the parents of that child would do whatever it took to destroy the school. As much as it broke his heart, he had decided it would be better for all the people who depended on the school if he just let them have their way.

Shawn was very mature about it and refused to spare a glance for the principal as he walked out of the office and took his son out of the building. He hadn't given in to the very primal urge to rip the spines out of the lawyers that held the fate of dozens of people in their palms. In retrospect, if he hadn't been worried about who would care for his son if he did, he likely would have done something close to that very thing before happily going to jail.

Finding himself back in the present, he looked up from the papers to see his son sitting there looking at him, still silent and contempla-tive. He looked at the clock and saw that he'd kept his son longer than normal with the absolute bomb he'd dropped.

"You can check that out after your show today," he said softly, urging his son out of his stupor. "You're late, son. Sorry for telling you right before your show." He'd said the words as calmly as he could, but he wouldn't ever be able to put into words how much it hurt him inside having to tell his son he was dying. He'd have rather gone out quick, but life went the way it went.

He watched as his son got up from his chair, cursing under his breath as if Shawn couldn't hear the expletives. He kept watching as his son set himself to rights before leaving his father sitting there in a chair, watching... always watching his son and the man he'd become.

A few minutes later, as he sat in his chair, he felt the hair on the back of his neck stand and he began to look around, feeling like he was being watched. He thought he heard a slight peal of devious laughter from somewhere, but couldn't quite place it. He dismissed it and relaxed back into his chair after looking around.

Shawn wasn't quite sure what to do with himself now that his son had been told about what was going to happen. He wanted to find something constructive to do, but there wasn't a single thing on his mind that needed doing.

After spending a few minutes contemplating the reality of his situation, he decided to do what he normally did and grabbed his phone, tuning in to the website he watched his son livestream on with their friends. It was time for the next episode of their show. He looked down and sighed a little as he watched his boy and his friends together and knew that the next few months might be easier for him than for his son.

He'd gotten to a point where he was accepting the inevitable, but his son had just learned, and had the terrible job of having to tell his friends. He wasn't sure what Caellum would do about his affairs during this time, but he was sure he would get through it... eventually.

He got up slowly from his chair and noticed that his posture had been terrible lately, as if he couldn't manage the desire to sit up straight like he had for most of his life. He grimaced to himself in distaste and annoyance. He wasn't that broken yet, and he knew it. At least, he thought he did.

Shawn walked into his living room and set up his laptop near him, as was his habit, to keep watching his son out of the corner of his eye. He looked amusedly at his guilty pleasure, sitting on the tray, "The Adventures of Jetpack 'Jimmy' Jingleheimer," It was a serial release harem story about a cripple who saved the day and got all the girls.

The cover looked like a comic book and a pulp fiction story similar to Indiana Jones, that had a baby. On his table was Issue 1, "The Name of Jingleheimer." His mouth twisted a little as his newest guilty pleasure would likely be short-lived. He'd barely get to read the first three or four issues before he was gone, he imagined.

Setting aside a story he'd never get to the end of, he walked over to the TV he kept and then set up his N64, determined to get through another couple of replays of his favorites, and today, Zelda was calling his name like a sweet siren's song on an ocarina.

As he sat, playing while watching his son's livestream, he felt that same familiar prick at the back of his neck, like he was being watched. He hadn't felt that way in... perhaps thirty years that he could recall. It was a hell of a note to feel it again now.

Every time he felt it, he glanced up to the ceiling, or the corners of the room, as it felt like whatever it was, was looking down on him from somewhere. He wasn't religious, so didn't believe it was anything divine. It couldn't be anything evil, for that matter, either. But no matter what he did, he couldn't shake the feeling that something far, far beyond him, was watching.

Chapter 3

A few months had passed with nothing changing of note. Caellum made more time to visit when he wasn't too busy, but he still kept living at his own home, though Shawn was sure that it wouldn't last. IF he knew his son, he was fairly certain he'd move back in when Shawn finally succumbed to how weak he felt.

He had done a great job of keeping up his health and acting as if nothing had happened, and he'd done a great job of rolling with the changes as they had happened. A few of them were overkill in his mind, but his son and friends insisted he cooperate.

After his son had told his friends about what he referred to as "his condition," they had made a move he hadn't expected of them. They'd canceled their contract with the building they shot their show out of. Rather than work there, the entire team had relocated to his basement, telling him it was more cost-effective. It might be true, but he just didn't have the heart to call "bull" to their flimsy reasoning.

They had, in fact, moved to their current studio from his basement to begin with, as soon as they were able to afford it with the money they were making. Now that they made even more, he knew without a doubt that their coming back to his basement had nothing to do with money. It was all about him, and he could say that without a shred of doubt or arrogance.

It was actually quite a blast from the past to have them back. It was mostly the same crew, even down to the lighting and editing. As he had done in the past, he watched while the crew performed and even made a few special guest appearances. He was thankful that no one had said on camera that he was dying, although they had said that they were likely going to go on a hiatus for a while after a few more real-life events happened. He knew it was code for "when Shawn kicks the bucket."

Shawn had actually missed having the adorable little bastards in his home all the time, though he'd never tell them, refusing to justify their over-the-top actions. It was nice for him to see them all grown up and doing well for themselves. Each of them now owned their own home in a part of the country. Many had struggled just to pay rent before, and now they'd each done it before turning thirty.

That wasn't the only change they'd implemented, however. They had insisted on one of those silly motored devices that let him sit in a chair while it ascended and descended the stairs for him. He didn't use it, but wasn't dumb enough to think he never would. They had also raided his refrigerator. It was the one thing he'd genuinely fought over. He *needed* real food.

Where once his kitchen had boasted milk, eggs, bacon, a few microwave dinners for emergencies, some vegetables like mushrooms and squash, and his much beloved steak. He even usually had some kind of fruit to snack on. All in all, he was a fairly healthy person with a few luxuries he refused to give up, including ice cream.

That said, the adorable little bastards he'd helped raise had invaded his home again, and they had destroyed the kitchen he'd loved. Now stocked with foods he previously wouldn't touch with a ten-foot pole. His son somehow guilted him into choking down foods like kale and tofu, now that he wasn't cooking for himself anymore. Every time he went to start cooking, one of the jerks he loved like an adoptive child started doing it for him.

He was drinking every type of health crap on the market, and it was making him very aggressive. He really just wanted actual food. It was unfortunate that he couldn't quite digest the wide array of foods he used to love because of their grease or sugar content. He'd joked a week ago that he'd kill his son for a Klondike bar, or his little friends for a single slice of bacon.

It was the intent of each of the kids, that he would live as long as possible, but he really just wanted to live how he used to, ignoring his body's protest every time he ate or drank anything it didn't agree with. Even with the dietary changes and the way the kids were helping to take care of him, he still kept losing weight.

It felt like he lost more each day, and where he was once a robust man, he felt skinny and weak, and his scale said the same. He had lost nearly 45 lbs. in the three months since he'd told his son. And felt like he actually needed the railing on each staircase as he walked up and down. If it continued much longer, he knew he'd have to give in to the damned chair on the stairs the kids had installed.

He had gotten to do one thing he hadn't expected. He had gotten to go to a hockey game with his son again. They'd gone to Anaheim to watch a game, which was a whole day trip, but worth it. The game was so much better live than it ever was on TV. Caellum had taken over that day, and had bought them both matching jerseys, much like he'd once done for his son as a kid.

This time, before taking the terrible picture, his son had put him on his shoulders to make a point. It was funny at the time and he'd laughed, but in hindsight it really put into perspective the stark reversal in their roles at this point in his life. He wasn't anywhere close to being prepared for the emasculating experience that was sitting on his son's shoulders.

He hadn't mentioned it and was absolutely certain he hadn't let his emotion slip to his son, but it broke his heart to rely on his son like that. Although, it swelled at the same time, knowing he'd raised the kind of man who would go out of his way to try to make his father's last few months of life memorable. He knew he'd done something right as he looked at the pictures side by side in his car; one of him taking his son to a hockey game, and now the one of his son taking him.

That was also the last day he'd eaten real food, and honestly, that cheeseburger had been one of the best things he'd ever eaten, especially when paired with his favorite beer. That had sat in his stomach for a couple of hours, but the grease and other ingredients had him puking on the side of the road as they'd driven home. It had been worth it, he'd thought, just to be normal. Sadly, *that* was the day they'd annihilated his kitchen.

Now, he tended to move around in and around his home, trying to spend as much time under the sun as he could while he was still able to move under his own power. At one point, he'd been able to maintain a level of physical activity, but with each little bit of weight he lost, he could feel both his strength and stamina drain. He honestly didn't know how much longer he'd be mobile.

When it happened, he was going to be giving out some apologies to the kids, because he knew from memory that he was a terrible patient. He hadn't had long enough with his wife, but he remembered her leaving the room when he was sick, just so she wouldn't be a target, only to turn around and do the same thing when she got sick.

He grinned at the memories of her, and if he had any happy thought in his mind, it was a hope that wherever the human consciousness ended up, hopefully he'd get to see her again. He'd never remarried, and honestly hadn't ever regretted it as he'd raised his son. He never had to split his focus on anything other than work, and while it had been hard... And it was damned hard at times to make ends meet... It had been the most rewarding thing in his life.

As he thought about his wife, he decided to stop being a lay-about and actually get something done. It was probably too late for a lot, but there were some things he could set in motion. He was fairly certain that when he died, his son wouldn't want to keep this home of his. He was also fairly certain he wouldn't have any money and the house would have to be sold just to cover some of the medical and funeral expenses, not to mention anything else he had to do.

He looked back at his papers and smiled a little, finding again the two sheets of paper that he'd tried to give his son. In all the excitement lately, and all the changes, he hadn't quite managed to pin his son down to give them to him and actually have him look at them. He might have to incorporate some help, and thought his son's friends could chip in a little... eventually.

He grabbed some papers around him and began drafting something he hadn't done in a long time for himself. He began to draft a story for his son and friends to play in their game. It wouldn't be anything too long, but he had a feeling Caellum would appreciate not having to be a full-time writer once in a while. Besides, he'd always liked his father's stories.

He decided that rather than give his son the character sheet with the intent to have him play with it, he'd make a new character and do his best to incorporate it into the story that he'd have Caellum play for him. He thought about it a lot and decided he'd do his best in the role of a teacher or a leader, or some other old man archetype.

Wisdom would be the name of his game, and hopefully, his son would take something away from it. Something like, 'you can't punch your way through all of your emotions, kid,' or something like that. He wasn't anymore blind than his son as he'd noticed that his son had also been losing weight, but it looked like he was preparing for a cage match, and his muscles had become more pronounced as Shawn had gotten weaker.

After writing a fair portion of the story he'd wanted, which really didn't take as long as people made it out to, he decided he'd done all he could for the day. He set down his pencil, still enjoying the feeling of physically writing things, and felt his neck prick up again, like it had before. It was happening a lot lately and he could never place where it came from.

At the feeling, he made another important decision, before he was too weak to make certain decisions for himself. He pulled out a post-it note that had a few special numbers on it and began to dial them one at a time. It was time for a meeting to get everything set up.

Shawn picked up his cell phone, which felt heavier lately, like everything else seemed to, and called his doctor, "Hey doc, it's Shawn."

He heard a deep breath get taken in from the other end of the phone as the doctor heard him. "What's up Shawn?"

He looked at the ceiling, taking another glance around the room for the culprit, futile as it always seemed. A cynical and slightly superstitious part of him wondered if it was death looking at him and telling him, 'soon.'

"I need a favor," Shawn said, getting right to his point. "I'm getting everything together and I could use a friend to help. Can you make some time for me?"

Chapter 4

Everything went largely as he'd expected. He'd gotten in touch with his lawyer, his doctor, and eventually they had gotten everything taken care of for his impending death. If he were being honest with himself, he would have admitted that the most terrifying part of this entire process was the acceptance.

He'd come to terms with his own mortality, and accepted his certain demise in no less than a couple more months. While Shawn had been up front with his son about most everything that had happened, he wasn't so good with the details of some of it. He knew himself well enough to admit he wasn't a details man when it came to law or medicine and trusted his professional help with those.

It was why, when they finished putting all the details together, he had decided to let his lawyer tell his son. He was getting tired and honestly didn't want the agitation that came with an argument. His energy was too valuable to waste on something like that.

His room was the last thing to change in his home, but there was no mistaking when it did. Gradually, as time passed, he spent much more time sleeping and resting than he had previously. Eventually they had decided that he needed a cane, then a wheelchair both upstairs and downstairs as his muscles began to deteriorate.

When it was time for the wheelchair, and he realized he was in bed somewhere around seventeen hours a day, he had 'the talk' with his doctor and friend. It was time for the hard decisions, after all, while he could still make them. His son was with him almost every waking hour, now, that he wasn't shooting his show or just trying to stay in shape.

One of the last things he'd done before being condemned to his wheelchair was browbeating his son into looking seriously into an offer from a game company. *Dreamscape Gaming,* he thought they were called. He wanted to know that his son would keep going, even when it was hard when he was gone.

As he understood it, they gave his son a hell of a contract offer for the near future, and had taken on his entire operation to prepare for a massive project. He was sure it would take a couple of years to complete, and he thought his son would have a handle on his attitude by then, if not sooner.

There was another problem, although it wasn't one he could really help with. His son had been dating a girl for a while now, and while he had been healthy, things had seemed to be progressing fine. Although he'd had to deal with the knowledge, his son would never move quickly enough that he could watch him get married before he passed on.

Now that he wasn't fine, though, his son was acting like he knew he would, but this girl hadn't been prepared for the attitude Caellum was demonstrating. They had started fighting, which broke his heart a little, at what she took to be his lack of emotion. He'd tried saying something, but she had changed the subject when it had come up and he knew he wouldn't be able to help.

At the same time, he knew his friends were about to drop a bomb on his son he couldn't prevent from happening. He knew he probably only had a month, maybe two, left. To that, he'd made the choice to refuse further treatment and submit to hospice care. They'd be around in the next couple of days to set up. They would make sure he wasn't in pain and was comfortable, but that was all there was left.

He'd spoken with his lawyer and left directions for everything that was supposed to happen. He just hoped that in his potential last few weeks alive, his son didn't treat him any differently than he had before. He was proud that his son had done a great job of treating him like normal thus far, though he was aware it hurt his son deeply to see him like that.

He had had a conversation with his son a few weeks previous that stuck with him. He had been sleeping when his son came to visit from his own home, and Shawn hadn't missed the small ways in which his son had begun to change. He'd changed in larger ways, too. As Shawn's condition worsened, his sons' condition seemed to improve. He'd been a large man before, like his father. He'd been mostly muscle and carried himself a bit like a bodybuilder without having to put in the work.

Now, however, he'd slimmed down as well, losing a couple of very important inches from his body, which changed him from a body-builder to a fighter. Shawn was a little concerned about what would happen if Caellum got into a fight with someone with how he looked. His eyes were those of a predator.

Even so, he was still the same to Shawn, still the son he'd raised, even if he looked like a caged animal at times, unable to sit still and waiting for something he could kill to come along. He'd woken up from his sleep, seeing all of this in his son, and heard him playing the music he had grown up with, and some he'd found on his own on the guitars that were now in Shawn's room.

He'd told his son what he could of the arrangements he'd made for his passing and had sworn he could have heard his son's jaw crack; he'd clenched it so hard. Despite the tension in he could see in his son's body, Caellum didn't miss a note as he kept playing his song. To Shawn's delight, Caellum had clearly put in time to learn the song properly.

"I tried to give this to you a few months ago," he said. "Stuff happened, and well, you left it behind." He pulled out the two pages he had attempted to give his son, and handed them over directly this time, refusing to allow them to be forgotten, "You might remember this, or you might not; but it's yours."

He watched his son look at the character sheet of the first character he'd ever called his own, long before he'd learned how much dice hated his very soul. His son went over it line by line, parsing out the information with eyes used to looking at such papers now.

He noted how his son's eyes lit with slight memories he hadn't thought of in years, and for a moment, father and son sat in a kitchen together twenty years younger. "Remember how to read that?" he'd asked. His face had brightened a little with this topic.

"I think so. How long have you had this, dad? Actually, explain these stats to me, so I know I've got it right." Shawn spent the next few minutes explaining it to his son.

"It isn't all that different than most tabletop games out now," he said. "The only real interesting changes to most modern tabletop games were a combined mental statistic and the addition of a new one: Soul."

Shawn believed that every living person, with some exceptions here or there, had the ability to channel magic into something they held dear for one reason or another. It was how some items became treasures when they might instead only be trash.

"For a farmer, that could be a hoe or a rake, where a warrior might find a sword or their armor unreplaceable." Shawn nudged his shoulders in what barely passed for a shrug. "At least, I believed that it was an interesting idea for a tabletop game. As for the combined mental statistic, it has to do with a dislike of quantifying the abilities of the human mind in numbers."

"Attempting to quantify wisdom and intelligence separately has a tendency to disallow inspiration, which sucks when attempting to garner character development." He smiled, "the last thing that you might have noticed is there is no system for experience. After all, that wolf should be able to kill you no matter what level you are if it rips out your throat."

They spent a couple of hours going over the papers before Shawn looked over to Caellum and saw a flash in his son's eyes. He'd recognized the pending exhausted sleep he was getting close to again. He'd made a face when his son got up and opted to make him dinner. "I'll get some food ready for you, Dad," he said, walking out of the room.

He didn't catch the look Shawn had as he walked out the door, or the chill Shawn felt, like the one he'd felt months prior. He looked up to the corners again for some sign of what that tickle at his senses could be, but sank back into his pillows instead.

Something in the back of his mind knew he'd find out eventually what that feeling was.

As Shawn sat in his bed, he could hear the discussion happen below him, and though the voices were fairly quiet, he heard the conversation through the vents. He knew his son had never discovered how many sounds traveled to his room upstairs.

It was a good thing, honestly, because Shawn knew a lot more about his son than he'd ever wanted to; as a teenager, especially when he'd thought he could get away with sneaking a girl into the house. Shawn's response to that experience had been to set a box of condoms on his son's dresser the next day.

For now, he heard that inflection of anger and the pain in his son's voice. He was too exhausted to make out the words, but he winced even as he faded into sleep at what he imagined his son was saying, and the stress of the situation.

The next few weeks were a blur to Shawn, as things progressed quickly for him. He didn't require much as he got weaker, but he felt the call of the grave approaching. He found himself, not for the first time, asking himself if there was anything he could or would like to do for everyone he was leaving behind, but he hit the wall of his fairly comprehensive will every time.

Shawn accepted the people in his home taking care of his needs, so that his son could get some alone time. He noticed how his son didn't spend much time with his girlfriend, but didn't ask after it. He wouldn't be able to help much there, anyway. He also noticed that his son had slimmed down even further in the weeks that followed.

He managed to make it through the first week of July before he needed help to function. He became too weak to leave his bed at all, and his son only left his bedside to shower when he was asleep. They spoke of normal things, but Shawn could tell that there was a lot of life his son wasn't living just to spend the couple of hours a day with his father he did.

He hated it, but he was grateful his son was there. He was the only person Shawn had in the world to call his own, and he was going to be sad to leave. It wasn't as if he had much choice, but he was going to be sad about it. He had enough time and wits about him to finish one more run of a favorite video game, although he was required to play it on easy so he wouldn't exert himself.

***

On July 13, Shawn Wraine died in his sleep. He was unfortunate enough to watch his soul rise out of his body in time to see the look on his son's face just after his last couple of breaths left his chest in a rattle. He knew the experience of watching his father die would stick with him. Two days later, he was buried at a cemetery in a wooden casket with a black marble headstone.

It read: In Loving Memory of Shawn Wraine. October 17, 1968 - July 13, 2019. The epitaph read, "May you live on in the things you create."

Chapter 5

Shawn stood vigil over his funeral, looking at everyone who had come out for it. Some faces he'd expected, while others were a massive shock. He was happy to see the volume of people that had come to celebrate his life, and there was a face he hadn't seen in over twenty years.

He recalled it as if it had only happened a few days ago, and it had haunted his mind for years. He saw the principal who had expelled his son at the age of ten, though the man looked as if he were on his own deathbed. He had looked in his middle age when Shawn had met him, just over the hump of forty or so at a glance.

While Shawn had expected him to look older, he hadn't expected the man to look nearly eighty. He watched as the man passed by his casket with a tear in his eyes and apologized to Shawn's body, much the same way he had then, only this time with a lot more emotion.

He apparently had quit the school district after that year, Shawn found out a couple of years following his move. He'd retired early and gotten a job as a painter, unable to stomach the idea that he'd failed to protect a child so spectacularly as he had Caellum Wraine.

Shawn felt a little twist to his guts, an odd feeling for a spirit, as he thought of this man who'd also suffered doing the best he could in a horrible situation. The man passed and Shawn continued to watch as person after person walked by his casket, throwing a small fistful of dirt or setting a flower on top of the wood.

He saw his son walk by without a tear in his eyes. Shawn could see past that though, and looked into his son's pain and deep sadness. It was something that would probably take a fair bit of time to get over. He was sorry for that, but had decided months ago to let his son muddle through on his own… It was the only way he'd grow.

He saw his son's friends one by one come through, each setting a rose on his casket, many crying. Even as a spirit, he choked up a bit watching them, unable to say anything, as he felt just a little pride in helping so many kids reach for their dreams, and leaving such a mark on their lives.

His boss even showed up and apologized for working him too hard and taking him for granted. It had apparently been very hard to find people to replace him and he'd had to hire two people to do it. When everyone had passed, he saw his son was still there, watching as the casket was lowered into the earth and filled in.

When the ground was full, and after his son finally left, he watched the air around him move with a slight breeze he could no longer feel. As he took in a breath he didn't need, he saw something materialize out of the surrounding air. Though through a series of ripples created by the surrounding shadows, an enormous form began to materialize and solidified.

It was the form of a humanoid, but unlike anything he'd expected to see. It looked like… a panda? He'd expected the grim reaper, a being made of bones and shadow, covered in a cloth and holding a scythe. Instead, he was looking at a damned panda. He focused on the bizarre features of the bipedal bear as he finished coming together:

The panda was standing on two legs, as one might have seen if they'd ever watched a certain trailer for an expansion to a MMORPG.

Except the fur wasn't short, like on one of those animated creations. Its fur was long, like a golden retriever, and looked rough and worn. The white fur matted with black, different hues, and sections of hair clumped together in spots, as if the panda had gone through filth and hadn't been groomed in a long time.

He was tall, towering over Shawn, and dressed distinctly in Asian clothing. If he were to put a style to it, it was like looking at the stereotype of a samurai... just a panda instead of a man. He had on a straw hat, which looked as if it had seen better days. There were multiple chunks missing from it, though none were important enough to ruin the hat completely. He had what looked like a piece of wheat in his mouth, which he obviously chewed. On closer inspection, Shawn amended that, deciding it was more likely a bamboo shoot.

He was garbed in a kimono like a traditional Japanese warrior may have worn, and it looked to have one time been an exquisite piece of clothing, but it saw disrepair and wear that made it look ragged. At his sides were a pair of swords, one short and one long, whose scabbards were black, plain, and unpolished, as if they'd needed care a decade ago. Shawn couldn't see the feet of this monstrous creature before him, but wouldn't have been surprised to see traditional footwear, any more than it would surprise him to see the panda barefoot.

Without preamble, he began to laugh. It was too absurd. *This* was the grim reaper? Granted, he didn't look like a fluffy little cuddle bear like the one he'd seen at the zoo. Even so, this was absurd. Perhaps it was just how abhorrently depressing the last few months had been for him, but for the first time in ages he laughed until he felt a tear in his spirit. He doubled over like he still had a body and couldn't breathe, the habits of a lifetime compelling his actions and reactions.

He watched as the bear expelled air in a huff and only laughed harder. He couldn't seem to help himself. He watched while the reaper eyeballed him for a few seconds before chuffing a little and pulling out the shorter of his two swords.

Shawn laughed straight through the panda disappearing over his body for a moment, looking at the top of the spirit's skull as he hovered. Shawn presumed the panda used his sword to cut the strings tying his soul when he felt his spirit fly free of the links binding him to his earthly body. Without having much time for anything but his laughter, he felt the world go black once more, as it had when he first passed.

Shawn came to on a small boat; one he would have described as being like a gondola. Rather than a sense of calm as he might have otherwise felt while rocking as if in a cradle, he felt his lips curl up in a smile. He had seen a damn panda acting as the grim reaper. It was perhaps the funniest thing he'd seen in a year.

At the rocking of the boat, he levered himself up to his knees and turned over, coming to a sitting position on the floor of the boat. He lifted his head up to look at the same panda who had appeared before him at his grave. He was proud of himself for not laughing anymore, but he couldn't help the mile-wide smile plastered to his face looking at his reaper.

When he peered out over the side, he saw clean water with a faint fog covering it, and he noticed gray all around him, as if fog encircled them on all sides. He sat back with that same smile unmoving as they floated along, pushed by a large stick the panda used to propel them forward through the water. Hanging off a hook from the front of the boat, a single lantern attempted to pierce the blanket of fog.

Shawn watched with passive interest as they finally passed through the fog, and he saw more docks than he could count, one after the other. He and his gondolier picked one, and they came in so smoothly

Shawn couldn't even hear the tap of wood on wood as the boat came into contact with the dock.

Shawn got to his feet and followed the panda as he disembarked the boat, noticing how it didn't seem to rock at all as they left. His humor was enough that he didn't have any of the questions he'd once thought he might when dying. He didn't question if he'd lived well enough, didn't ponder the existence of an afterlife of any kind, and didn't ponder if he would do anything different given a chance.

He did, however, note to himself how bizarre it was to find he didn't care about anything like that. With a shrug, he stepped off of the dock and followed the escort he had down a pathway leading towards a resplendent building in the distance. After walking for a time, he came to a plaza, large enough for a few thousand people to gather, which had branching paths leading off in every direction.

His reaper chose one off to the right and they began their journey towards what he assumed might be the castle. He went through the twists and turns along the path without much of an issue, although he reached a hill, he found particularly difficult to climb after a while. As he walked up it, he recalled making the decision to leave his home with his son.

After he climbed up the hill, he found there were a couple more leading upward, though each was significantly smaller than the first. He found himself recalling having to find work in a new place, getting his son enrolled in school, and doing his best to make ends meet. He was lucky to have had enough money to purchase their home outright, although it left him with not much extra for anything else. It turned out his home in Minnesota had been worth more than he'd thought.

Shawn thought about all the decisions he'd made in his life, from deciding to help his son's friends get started to having to tell his son he had cancer. Some of these came while he was walking uphill, but quite a few also came when he walked downhill. The path was convoluted, but he dutifully followed the bear along it, eventually coming to a door.

The door was simple, yet extravagant in its size. It could easily fit five of him side by side, and he wasn't small either. The panda looked back at him for a moment and walked into the building after nodding his head, beckoning Shawn forward behind him. He followed.

He entered a room where he saw a large table with enough seating for fifty. At the end of it sat a single woman, likely the most beautiful he'd ever seen, with the exception of his wife, for obvious reasons. She had dirty blond hair that trailed down her back in a single ponytail, bright green eyes set in a narrow face, and an athletic figure that had just enough curves to interest a man.

As Shawn looked at her, he found some features were similar to his deceased wife, but dismissed it as coincidence. She wore a simple yet elegant blue dress that was fit to her form. Aside from that, she had a smile on her face that stretched as far as any he'd seen when alive, as if his presence made her happier than anything else on Earth could have.

Her eyes ran up and down Shawn as he walked up to her, taking in everything he was with a sweeping and piercing stare. As she looked down the length of him her smile stayed on her face, but as she looked into his eyes and finished her assessment of him, he watched her eyes flash with an emotion he would have labeled as alarm, although it was gone as quickly as it had come. For that single moment, it was there. Shawn had the distinct impression he should run away; fast and far.

Her hand sat frozen in midair, gesturing to the chair in front of her for Shawn to sit in, and he took his seat, noticing that his escort had suddenly vanished from the room and feeling a dramatic shift in the atmosphere that had been here when he'd taken his first steps into this room.

Interlude

"What the fuck?" said Elegy, her voice coming out as both a growl and a squeak. Clenching her teeth, she seethed with the new information.

She had stopped the time of this man named Shawn Wraine, and taken another appraising look at him, verifying what she'd seen those times in the months prior to his death. Her fears were well-founded and very real. The worst part? She couldn't do a single damned thing about it.

She spun to the silent companion at her side, words coming out in a flurry. "Did you see anything out of the ordinary when you went through his life?" The panda in question only shrugged while holding her gaze, which she interpreted to mean nothing was wrong. "Damnit, I thought we got rid of him! Why did he have to come back?"

The panda was bemused. He'd never seen his mistress yell quite like this. Now that he thought on it, as long as he'd been in her employ, he'd never heard her curse at all, or anything like what she was doing now. If he'd ever wondered what it would be like to see her lose her temper, he now had a point of reference.

Silently he watched as her rant continued, "Blew up the universe once and it's not good enough? If the other one comes back too, we are all screwed!" It amused him more than a little to watch such vulgarity come from her, and he felt that might be because her voice was so beautiful he couldn't have seen it... until he *had* seen it.

She looked upon Shawn's body again, scouring his memories, and finally seeing one in the back of his mind that she hadn't looked at before. It wasn't exactly an important memory, but it was one that probably started the whole damned train wreck about to happen to the universe and every plane on it.

Shawn was much younger, twenty-one or twenty-two in the memory. He didn't recall himself, so she couldn't see. He sat at a bar with friends, talking about hobbies and women, much like all people that age did. They weren't disrespectful, but interested. As hobbies went, they only had one real hobby that she could tell, even when looking at his entire life rather than one memory: tabletop games.

Shawn ran the game he and his friends played, but they were getting bored with stories other people made, and were trying to badger their friend into writing his own story and creating his own universe for his friends to explore. They had tired of everything being about dragons, orcs, goblins, elves, druids, and humans, and wanted more variety in their games. To do that, they needed Shawn's help.

Shawn thought about it while his friends changed the subject to talk about their recent experiences with women, and Elegy watched as he took an exceptionally long pull on his beer and got up from the table to use the restroom, needing to vacate his bladder so that he could drink more. When he walked into the bathroom, that was when she saw the blot on the world form.

Out of the shadows, he came into the otherwise empty bathroom. Remaining invisible, he appeared one grain at a time to her vision, and began to whisper in Shawn's ears. She could see a divine spark of insight being injected into Shawn by the form and grit her teeth hard enough she could have heard one crack if she were a mortal.

She watched through his memories, slowly, methodically, and clinically looking for any discrepancy that could give her a clue. Rather than seeing anything, she noticed that as Shawn developed his ideas for this new world, that shadow had been conspicuously absent from the memories. There wasn't a single dark blot of divine influence until the day Shawn had told his son he was going to die of cancer.

At that point, the blot showed up again and again, followed by Shawn almost noticing that he was being watched; and that was exactly what was happening. Shawn was being watched by the divine as he approached his death.

What gave her pause was that the majority of the moments this blot existed were when Shawn was thinking about the world he'd created, or when he'd been thinking of his son. Disregarding everything else on her schedule, Elegy single-mindedly searched for the answers to her various questions, finally coming to an answer that worried her more than she would ever admit.

Shawn had recreated the world of Aardia. True, he and his son had made it their own and there were many differences between the reality and the fictional, but it was here in the high-definition memory: That miserable bastard of a god Tethir was back. More importantly, he'd used a divine spark of inspiration on a mortal and had used him to bring to life a world they had agreed should remain closed for another few thousand years.

She didn't know what Tethir wanted exactly of the mortal standing in front of her, but it was clear he hadn't gotten it. What he had gotten though, was access to a world he was never supposed to so much as witness. How had he survived 'The Collapse?' She had to find out. Unfortunately, she was tied to this place, this job of hers, like any living mortal's soul was tied to their body. Only through avatars and champions could she extend her reach any further.

She sought within herself to find one of the few things she could accomplish alone. Glancing into the cosmos to the rest of the few living places in the universe, she discovered that each of them was still detached from every other planet. Exactly as they should be. Each deity observing them was maintaining an appropriate vigil, as they should.

As she continued to observe, she could see a world, previously dull and gray, lifeless and inanimate, starting to brighten with new life. All the gods who'd inhabited that world had gone dormant as well, and now a few of them were stirring. Across the cosmos, she could see a major shift beginning and needed to find a way to stop it.

She looked to the mortal in front of her for perhaps the fifteenth time since beginning this little internal quest of hers, as if looking for answers to a complex math equation. In a way, that's exactly what she was doing. She stomped her foot in frustration and growled again as she thought about potential solutions to the problem.

She began muttering to herself, as a man might when working alone on a car in a garage, "No, that won't work. I just need to... you, filthy bastard..." growling again she continued, "I can't... It won't. Ugh!" she said, finally exclaiming to herself at the end of the internal debate. She looked at her servant, still standing there and just watching the show, and looked right into his eyes.

"You can keep doing your job. You don't need to see where this goes, Patches." Hearing his nickname, the panda vanished in a flash, on his way to find another body to bring to the afterlife.

Elegy sat down in her chair again, finally coming to a conclusion she clearly hadn't wanted, knowing she had little choice in the matter anymore. It had to be done.

Chapter 6

S hawn sat in his seat and watched Elegy for a moment, not missing out on how robotic some of her actions were. She seemed to be struggling with something, although he had no idea what it was. Before he could put together the words to ask her what had so obviously messed with her natural rhythm, she spoke as if she'd forgotten something.

"Ah, everyone who comes to see me gets to eat a meal of whatever they'd like. Just imagine whatever type of food you would like and it will appear in front of you. You won't have any problems with digestion or anything like that, so take your pick of fantasy." Even though spoken as if just remembering her lines, she hadn't sounded unkind.

Shawn looked at her and decided everything else had been weird enough thus far that he would just roll with it. He gave it some real thought, taking her words at face value, before asking, "What about a drink?"

"Yes," Elegy said, "You get a drink of your choosing as well. It doesn't even have to be only one, if you've a mind to try many different things here. Imagine it and it is yours."

Not needing any other questions answered, as he'd already decided on his food, Shawn went with the one thing he'd been craving for months. A big, beautiful, American cheeseburger. Like most Americans he liked his burgers large and juicy, in his mind he wanted a brioche bun, garlic aioli instead of mayonnaise, a large medium rare patty topped with cheddar cheese melting over it, lettuce, sautéed mushrooms and onion, and cherry tomatoes that popped with juice in his mouth as he took a bite.

It was exactly what he'd dreamed of, and the beer that appeared at the table with the rich and hearty food he ate was exactly the thing he'd wanted. As he ate, he watched the judge's apprehension wane little by little, and her smile came back, now less robotic than it had been for a moment.

By the time he finished, she again looked as relaxed as she had when he had walked in. Looking around as he took another pull of his beer, he asked, "Where did the panda go? He was here, and then he wasn't."

"He went back to work," Elegy said. "I did not want him here for the conversation I am about to have with you. It will be... unique, and the knowledge isn't meant for him."

Shawn looked at her, now full to bursting with the meal he'd eaten. It had been amazing, more so than any burger he'd ever had before. He felt ready to make any decision he could imagine coming up.

Elegy spoke again after meeting his gaze. "We'll start with the basics. My name is Elegy." She paused for a second. "I am what you might call the judge. I send souls to the afterlife they are destined to reach after judging their actions."

Shawn nodded, again taking everything at face value. He couldn't come up with a single reason she'd lie to him. Besides, he was already dead, after all. His nature was to take things as they came and work through any difficulty. Not seeing any, he continued to listen to her fantastic story.

"All souls are worthy of respect, and while I see you weren't re-ligious, you respected everyone you met, and seldom judged where it wasn't your place. I'd like to thank you for that attitude." Shawn nodded again, feeling like his response wasn't really necessary.

Elegy paused for a moment before continuing slowly, "Typically, I give souls three or four options when they reach the afterlife. Each eventually involves getting judged and passing on." *Typically?* Shawn thought to himself, though he didn't speak out that he'd caught that interesting word choice.

"They can be sent back to Earth to watch over their loved ones, which many do. Those are what mortals refer to as ghosts. Second, they could go to what the Norse referred to as a version of Valhalla, where souls can freely drink and fight and enjoy their afterlife as long as they'd like. Each will be judged when there is no more unfinished business wherever they wind up.

"Some souls just want to pass on, and I respect that, and send them through. I'm only telling you of the next option because it would have been an option for you. Some, like the panda who guided you here, have sympathetic souls and I offer employment with myself. They become soul reapers, learn some of the secrets of death, and are part of something greater while keeping most of themselves."

Elegy stopped, as if finding what she was about to say was difficult. She blew out a breath and spoke slower than ever, "You... get to learn... some of what..." She blew out another breath, "mortals weren't meant to." Her teeth clamped together, and she spoke through them in frustration. "Because," another sigh slipped through her teeth before she finished the statement with vehemence, "that *bastard* messed it all up. *Again.*"

He had no idea who this bastard was, but he felt a little sorry for him. This didn't seem like a good woman to piss off. Elegy visibly paused to gather herself after that brief outburst.

She cleared her throat and almost seemed to reset the conversation when she continued, "You know the world you imagined? Aardia, as you called it?"

He nodded a little, unsure of where she was headed. "Yes?" Shawn said slowly, drawing it out almost as if it were a leading question.

"Well, it is... it's..." Her voice sank down to barely a whisper, "R..." Shawn hadn't caught whatever the last word she'd said.

"It's what?" Shawn said, having an idea about the last word.

"It's *real*!" Elegy said, grinding her teeth together at having to tell him. "Like *really* real. You were given a divine inspiration when you were thinking about its creation."

Shawn thought about that for a moment. "Really? That's pretty cool." He sat back in his chair while Elegy stared at him.

"That's it?" Elegy said, asking dumbly, "You find out there's another world, a place where many planes came together, and it's... cool?"

"Yeah." Shawn said, nodding eagerly. "It's pretty neat to know it's an actual place. I do have some questions about it, for obvious reasons, but they don't matter if you won't tell me." His grin was wide with the knowledge that the place was real. It was honestly exciting to him.

Elegy shook her head, again trying to reset herself. It wasn't what she'd expected to hear. She'd seen he was laid back, but she hadn't really considered how deep his attitude ran.

"Whatever," Elegy said, continuing, "The important parts of the story are that the god that gave you this divine inspiration isn't even supposed to exist anymore. He and another god all but killed each other a few millennia ago. We froze the world in stasis after it developed a little, not wanting it to rejoin what was left of the universe.

"Now... now I fear it is awakening, and the god Tethir may be back. I see him in some of your memories, although I doubt, he knows I can see him." Her smile became predatory for a moment and he had a glimpse into the character she could be if she were inclined. For a moment it was absolutely terrifying, "Death," she started, "Brings all together, and in death nothing is safe from my eyes.

"I need to know... Would like to know, Shawn Wraine, if you would go to this world you helped to create and be brought back to life as my agent? I need someone familiar with it to navigate it and see if there are any signs of it awakening. If it isn't, it will be a quick trip and you can come right back. If it is waking... well... I'd like someone there who can stand up to one of the other gods for me.

"The ones we left there; some are benevolent. However, most are not a wonderful influence on the universe. The big takeaway is that if they are awakening, that world is going to rapidly become a war zone. If it escalates as it did in the past, this time it could consume what remains of the universe, and all the worlds and planes that inhabit it."

Shawn had some questions about this place for the goddess, as he now assumed she was, but they didn't matter. Although, what she was offering came up to a second chance at life, especially on a world he'd dreamed of for decades.

"Sign me up."

Part 2: Colin Young

The Butter Made Me Do It

Axis of Anarchy Publishing and Design

Chapter 1

Colin stood, looking at the papers in his hand with a twist of annoyance to his mouth. Administrative Leave, the subject line had said in the clean text and format of every email sent out since the 1990s. The translation: He'd shot a bank robber who had shot at him. There were multiple videos, camera shots from both the bank and an unknown number of cell phones, not to mention the body camera he'd had strapped on.

He was on the fast track at the precinct in Kansas City, Missouri, where he called home base. At the ripe old age of twenty-two, they had promoted him to detective. Realistically, it was by sheer chance he'd been on hand when the robbery had been going on, having gone to the bank to question a potential witness to the case he was working on.

***

"10-65 in progress at the U.S. Bank at 221 West Gregory Boulevard. Shots Fired. Unknown number of robbers. Two detectives on scene. Immediate Assistance Requested," Colin spoke into his radio from outside of the bank. He and his new partner had both pulled out their service weapons and waited for a response from the radio.

"Acknowledged, units are three minutes from your position. Stand fast," Colin and his partner nodded at each other, secure in the knowledge they wouldn't be alone for very long as the situation progressed. On the other hand, three minutes could be a long time, especially in a robbery... long enough even that the robber might be gone by the time they showed up, but there was nothing they could do.

Colin had heard the shots from inside of the bank location as they were leaving the car and they saw a man wearing a black hoodie and blue denim jeans holding court in the bank. He was waiting for the tellers to dispense him the money he had demanded of them.

All the people were on the floor of the bank with their hands over their heads, as he had clearly dictated they do. Colin could only see one man through the clear glass doors of the bank, but there might have been more.

Colin squinted his eyes, peering through the binoculars he habitually kept in the car: the robber was having the tellers load money into the backpack he had at his side. It was a cheap-looking backpack, and on closer inspection, Colin noticed that much of the man looked out of sorts, like he couldn't afford better clothes.

After the second teller finished filling up his bag with money, he started out toward the door. When the shots had gone off, everyone on the street had cleared to what they considered a safe distance. Considering the man had a gun, it wasn't safe at all if he could see them.

Colin waited a moment to see what the man would do, and saw that he'd begun making his way out. Colin and his partner had each taken cover behind the doors of their car, which they had parked perpendicular to the road, allowing each to stand by their door and look at the scene while having solid cover, assuming the robber was using regular bullets in whatever pistol he had.

Each man was wearing body armor, having grabbed it from the trunk when they heard the shots. Colin's partner Derek had slunk back to the trunk to retrieve their gear while Colin kept his eyes on the only exit of the bank.

Their gear on, they both watched for a development in the situation. There was a bicycle parked just outside the bank, lying against the stone on the side of the building. Much to the irritation of Colin, people had taken out their cell phones and were taking videos and photographs of the situation. Colin and his partner had a clear view of their target, but the people behind them made them skittish. They were honestly too busy to ask them to leave, even for their own safety. People were people, after all.

The man trotted out of the bank to hear Colin yell loudly, "Kansas City Police Department! Put your weapon down slowly and put your hands up!" His gun was trained on the man, who looked at him with shock, clearly not expecting him to be there. He stood for a moment, and Colin repeated, "Drop your weapon and put your hands up! I do not want to shoot!"

The man's eyes flicked between Colin and his partner, as if measuring them up in a second. Without a word or another second to process what was happening, the man took a shot at Colin. He felt the bullet raise his hair as the man took the opportunity of Colin and his partner ducking for a moment to go for his bicycle, but before he had done anything more than pick it up, Colin already had his service weapon and had discharged two rounds. One was aimed right at the head of the suspect, while the other was aimed at their body.

Colin heard a scream behind him as he watched two bullets collide with the man, ignoring it instead of the more obvious danger at the moment. The first bullet disappeared into the suspect's body while the other blew a small chunk of his skull apart from his head as he was leaning away to get on his vehicle. Colin reacted in time with his partner, with his partner going into the bank to check on the safety of everyone involved. Colin went to check the body.

He might have felt like checking for a pulse was a bit redundant, as he could see some of the man's brain leaking onto the pavement, but he had habits he followed. The man was dead, as he'd figured was obvious to anyone watching. He looked back at the crowd to see something he hadn't wanted to.

A small woman was lying on the ground, a pool of her own blood forming under her, from twenty feet behind where Colin had been standing. Colin raced towards her, already calling into his radio for assistance, "Civilian harmed at the scene, request emergency assistance, suspect neutralized."

He reached the woman but found that it was too late before he ever got to her. She was likely dead before she'd hit the ground. In the woman's hand was a cell phone, still recording the last moments of her life. "Change that, Code 10-45D, civilian deceased. Situation under control."

He cursed to himself once he'd let go of his radio. He sat there on his haunches, looking down at the dead woman. The bullet had punched right through her throat. He hoped she hadn't suffered too much—it had collided center mass and blown through her windpipe.

If only she hadn't been so interested in videotaping the robbery, she would likely still be alive now. Colin felt a chill as he remembered the bullet flipping his hair a little and thought about how lucky he had been. He wished the man hadn't shot at him and just let him arrest him. Now his life really was over.

Colin stayed at the scene, along with his partner. They had found that there was no one in the bank that had been harmed in the robbery. The man had fired his gun into the ceiling just to show that it was a real gun, like that would have been necessary to garner compliance from the bank workers.

He snorted, knowing bank workers were some of the most compliant people in active shooter situations in America. They were even the easiest people to rob, as efficient as they tended to be. Even thinking about how idiotic the man was didn't take his mind away from the woman in the street. She had looked young, with long brown hair and a small narrow frame. He remembered her eyes, a light blue glassed over in death and still open. He didn't touch the body once he'd determined her death, doing his best to allow the coroner and the CSIs to do their jobs properly.

The two of them stayed where they were, and when every other pertinent individual showed up, they went back to the precinct to be questioned in their own station. By the end, they had run through the story what felt like a hundred times and nothing changed in their accounts, no matter how they had to describe what had happened.

In the end, they placed Colin on administrative leave. The captain had even been nice enough to enclose his official leave notice in an email. It was overkill, but that was their captain, making sure there was a large paper trail behind him no matter what decisions he made.

Colin balled his fist in annoyance and, in a rare show of temper, he kicked the small trash can at his desk as he went to his locker to grab his gear and go home. He wasn't to show his face at the precinct for three days, no matter what happened, which meant at the very least he'd have to go to an actual gym to get a workout, rather than the facilities at his work.

He gave a fist bump to his partner, and they parted ways wordlessly from the police department, his partner going towards his car while Colin began the trek to his apartment on foot. At a normal walk, it took Colin about thirty minutes to get home, as he tended to stop along the way to converse with the people he knew.

Today he made it in less than fifteen, not stopping even once to have a conversation. He just nodded at people and wished them a good evening, as it was near closing time for everyone. He dropped his clothes at the door, refusing to go through his normal routine, and dropped into the single recliner he kept in his apartment, sinking into it as he sighed.

He knew he'd be thinking of that woman for days. The suspect who'd shot at him be damned, but he'd think of the woman who'd gotten shot just for being there for a while. He wasn't normally bothered by the odd death at his job, which he supposed made him a bit bizarre, but when innocent people died, it got to him.

It wasn't even a case he'd work, when everything was said and done. The guy who'd done it was dead, and the bank had gotten their money back. Even if they hadn't, they were very well insured, so it was a non-issue. That woman, though, she'd never get her life back. Feeling restless, Colin walked to his room and grabbed a change of clothes and threw them into his extra gym bag. He felt keenly the need to vent some frustration at the moment.

Colin spent the rest of his day at the boxing gym just a few blocks away from his home, doing his best to pound away the frustration of losing someone that day. He didn't fight or spar with anyone, preferring the heavy bag for the way he felt. His eyes were like hot green glass while he focused on each and every punch, from jabs to body blows that he laid into it.

The gym closed a few hours later, and he exhaustedly went back to his apartment just to pass out and hopefully process the day better tomorrow.

Chapter 2

Colin sat up in his bed, dripping with sweat that had long run cold. He had a flashback to the woman on the street that day, and he found himself running towards her, unable to stop the bullet from impacting with her body. He'd watched in slow motion as she had crumpled to the ground and bled out. She'd raised a hand towards him on the way down, as if asking for help.

He looked at the digital clock next to his bed and with a grunt noticed it said, three A.M. It was always the way, that if someone had something on their mind as they passed out, three in the morning was when they'd wake up to stew about it some more.

With a sigh, he levered himself out of bed and got ready for a shower. He needed one, after all, to go with the new set of sheets he would need to replace the absolutely drenched ones on his bed right now. He dropped the boxers he'd worn to bed on the floor and padded his way over to the bathroom, where he stopped in front of the mirror to take a look at himself.

He looked thinner than he wanted, but what he had was well defined and muscular. His hair was a bright blonde, slightly bleached from the sun he saw with regularity, and cut short to accent his narrow face. His eyes looked back at him through the mirror and saw a slight red tint to them in a face that looked slightly sunken.

It made sense when he considered the stress he was feeling. He looked again at his face, contemplating that it was probably that same stress that made him look drawn and tired. The rest of his body was very toned, with little fat at all to speak of. He kept himself in shape by constantly playing sports with his friends and working out often.

Where he was incredibly strong and disciplined in his work life, his home life was much the opposite. He wouldn't have defined himself as messy, but neither was he organized. He knew where everything was, and that was the important part as far as he was concerned.

He ignored the bathroom scale he typically stood on each morning and went straight for the cold spray of water he'd desperately wanted. He felt disgusting now that he was awake. The icy water gave his body a jolt of adrenaline, immediately waking him from what little stupor he'd been feeling.

He let the water sluice over his skin as he seemed to replay both his dream and the day over and over again. Perhaps, he thought with a sigh, his three days of administrative leave were more necessary than he'd have admitted to anyone else. The troublesome part was the psyche evaluation he had to take part in before he could come back to full duty. He was scheduled to see the shrink on retainer with the police department the morning he was to return.

If they gave him a clean bill of health, he could go back to his normal duties. Colin doubted whether anything he'd been working on would still be an open project when he got back. After all, he was only one of a half dozen very qualified and competent people who could get the job done. He had left very detailed notes about his progress on the case he'd been working so there really wasn't much else he could do.

He smiled a little, curious about what kind of case they'd have him working on next. It was the only thing in his life that seemed to give him any genuine joy, as he was doing what he'd always wanted to, helping protect the peace and put bad guys behind bars, if not in the ground like the day before.

Colin got out of the shower and toweled off, not caring that his hair and skin were still a little damp. At three-thirty in the morning, he did what he hadn't done in three or four years. He called his mother to chat.

"Hey mom. How's it going?" He asked, starting the conversation as he did all others.

Colin heard lips smack across the line briefly before an answer came, "You all right, my baby?"

He smiled at the response, "Yeah, I'm good, mom. I just realized I haven't talked with you in a while and wanted to hear from my amazing mother."

"Don't try that with me, mister." He could almost see the frown form on her face as she spoke. "No one calls their mother at this god-awful hour unless something's up. Now I'm up too... So spill it, kid."

So much for lying about his mental health. "Well, see, there was this thing today and I kind of got sent home on administrative leave for a few days. Paid vacation?"

"Yeah? What happened? Did you screw up?" She asked, in a mother's way of sounding both caring and accusatory.

"I kinda..." he paused, "Shot a bank robber today. It was closer than I'd have liked." As he spoke the words, it occurred to him that in his haste to worry for the dead woman he'd nearly forgotten, he himself had nearly been shot in the head.

"Hmm..." It made him nervous when she didn't elaborate on the humming noise for a moment. "I knew I didn't like you leaving to become a big city cop."

"You didn't like it then, so why should that change, mom? I still like the difference I'm making here, even if you don't enjoy seeing me in danger. On the bright side, it'll be Wednesday before I go back to work, so take that as a win."

"You nearly got shot to get that time. It doesn't sound like a win to me." He heard her sniff delicately. He was damned if she didn't have a point. He didn't have a rebuttal.

"Are you doing ok, mom?" He hoped she'd let him change the subject.

"Don't think I didn't notice that," Damn, she always was a shrewd woman, he thought, "but I'll allow it because I love you. I'm fine. Just working like I do. Up all night most of the time and doing my best with it. I'm still not quite used to sleeping alone."

It surprised him she'd let that slip. Three years ago, just before he'd moved to Kansas City, his father had gotten killed in a drunk driving accident. It had been some stupid kid driving too fast with enough alcohol in his system to put down a bull. He'd offered to bring his mother with him, or even to stay, but she wouldn't have any of it, swearing that his father would want to see him live his dreams.

"Sorry, mom." He didn't have much else to say to her on the subject, "I miss him, too." That was the absolute truth. His father had been his principal support in convincing his mother to stop trying to browbeat him into being a small-town cop and eventually sheriff.

"Don't you worry about me. I'm keeping busy." She sighed a little, "So long as I know you're doing fine, I'll be happy, even if I don't like how you're doing it." Her voice took on an edge that even four hundred miles away had him quaking a little in reflex. "But if you get hurt, I will make you regret it, mister."

He laughed nervously at her before responding, "I won't. Just gonna take a few days to decompress."

"Alright," she said in a tone or finality. She continued in a much more tender voice, like the one she'd had when he'd first called, "Be safe, my baby. I love you."

"Love you too, mom. You be safe too. Let me know if you need anything." She hung up before he could add anything else, clearly not interested in anything but his happiness. It might have been rude, but that was his mother, through and through. Equally loving and the biggest hard-ass he'd ever known.

He sat down in the recliner, setting his cell phone on the table next to it. He passed out in the chair, unwilling to take the effort to change his bed, and finally slept dreamlessly.

***

The next day, he found himself doing whatever he could to keep busy. He was functioning much better than he had the day before, and had started by changing out his sheets and putting new ones on his bed. He'd taken the old ones over to his washer and tossed them in, deciding that he didn't get out enough and he'd go do something with the time he had.

A couple of hours later, dressed in blue denim jeans, a black t-shirt, and his beloved and scarred leather jacket, he found himself sitting down at a coffee shop he couldn't recall the name of. It wasn't a chain shop, because he honestly couldn't fathom supporting a corporation, given a choice. The girl who had taken his order had been cute and appeared to have been his age.

Against his typical behavior, he'd even flirted a little with the young woman, getting her to give him a smile as she sent him on his way to await his java. He sat patiently, watching people move, as was his habit.

One man was in a clear hurry, but wouldn't let that dissuade him from his fix. He was nice, even if in a near panic.

Another woman had walked up to get her order and found six cups, needing two trays to carry them all. Colin might have offered to help carry them to her car, but was afraid she'd take it wrong. It wasn't worth the chance, he'd decided pragmatically.

Finally, it was his turn to get his coffee, and he saw on the side of the cup the name and number of the woman who had taken his order. He looked at her and gave her a bright smile, now having to decide if he wanted to stay and chat on her break or leave. Deciding staying would likely hurt his chances, as she was quite pretty, he left and walked around with his coffee.

As he walked down the street, he pondered the cliché he'd just been part of and smiled slightly, deciding it amused him. He walked a few blocks down the road before deciding to buy a book. He wasn't much of a reader, but he had a few novels bumping around his apartment, usually from times where he had unplanned time to kill.

He walked into a used book shop, delighted to find a small collection of leather-bound Louis Lamoure novels, including Lonely on the Mountain, the last of the Sackett series, and one he had yet to read. If he recalled, he actually had most of Louis Lamoure's books in a series willed to him by his father, but he didn't have room in his apartment to bring them over yet.

Either way, he knew this one wasn't part of it, as he'd read every book in that collection his father had owned. It would be a book he could likely get through in his time off. He took what was left of his coffee, his new book, which had been at an outright steal of a price for the condition it was in, and walked over to a park bench, where he could hopefully enjoy the day in peace.

He took out a set of headphones and plugged them into his cell phone and played music, letting 1980s rock permeate his ears. None of these things were part of his typical habit, but he figured changing it up was working for him so far. He even managed to make it halfway through the book in the four hours he sat on the bench.

After a while, his rear end started getting cold, and it forced him to move or go numb. Colin dropped his cup into a nearby trash bin after typing the number into his phone and setting the receipt, which he had preserved in the book as a marker for some reason.

At home, he changed his laundry and looked up the name and number that had been left on his coffee cup from earlier. It was still too early to call if he was inclined to, so he got dressed in some shorts and a loose shirt and went down to the public basketball courts to find a game. There was *always* a game, if he was willing to play with the kids that showed up at this time. It didn't bother him at all.

He passed a few more hours this way before deciding he was done when his stomach growled. He'd done well. Better than some, but not as good as others, even if he was in better shape than most of the court. He just didn't have as much dexterity as the kids, who never stopped playing. They held the damn ball like it was glued to them.

He stopped by a taco truck to get some fresh food and was delighted at the steak tacos he'd ordered. Three of them were more than enough on a day like today. He ate in front of the truck before making his way home.

He even called Christine, the woman who had left her number on his cup, and he'd invited her out to dinner. He was all set to go out with her on Tuesday night before making his return to work. It would be a good weekend when it was over.

Chapter 3

Wednesday morning, he was given the all clear by the shrink, who'd asked him many more personal questions than he'd liked. He had nothing to hide, but still didn't like the probing inquiry. He imagined that getting to know the lovely Christine had helped his mental state dramatically, and he even had a second date planned with her on Friday evening, after he finished his shift.

His good cheer ended when he walked into the conference hall his boss used for morning meetings and found his next project staring him in the face, along with two members of the FBI. Up on the board was the project for the entire precinct. A serial killer who had changed locations had just been tagged in their fair city.

He was now in his third location, and the feds were really hoping to nail him here before more people got hurt. They'd nicknamed him 'The Iceman.' He always killed the same way, every time. It was his MO, or modus operandi. Every victim's cause of death appeared to be an icepick plunged into their temple. There was no weapon to pull prints from. All that remained was the hole in the temple, but the police in the other two cities had figured out he used an ice mold to make a new pick each time.

Unfortunately, that was one reason he was so hard to track, because he was methodical in many other ways. He favored younger women in their late teens or early twenties, always with the same build. He favored brunettes, who typically had a narrower face and his preference was for blue eyes, although one victim had green. Each also had a form that would have best been described as graceful in life. Each victim also had the appearance of a dancer, despite their day jobs.

In total, he had killed nine women, the last of which happening in Kansas City. Each woman also had bruising at the neck, indicative of being held down and choked as he used the pick to snuff out their lives.

They each worked a normal job that saw a lot of foot traffic, many worked in coffee shops or at fast-food restaurants. They'd gotten some footage together from the few places that had cameras up at the time and had been lucky enough that a few people who looked the same were in both cities at the time the footage had been taken.

They had a rough sketch of the man now. He was on the older side, probably in his late thirties or early forties, with light hair just now beginning to turn to gray. He had a lean face and appeared muscular, even though his dark clothes appeared a little baggy at both scenes. He'd worn glasses, and had a slight limp in his walk, favoring his left side just a little. At a glance, he was likely tall, appearing just over six feet in height. Given that, he was actually fairly attractive, if he weren't seen in the light of a serial killer.

Colin felt his juices flow at the man, finding himself a little excited to get a shot at a serial killer. He paused for a moment, checking his excitement. Should he really feel excited to be tracking down a murderer? It was worth thinking about, but only after he helped catch this man.

They all had their assignments around this case, from requesting that businesses like the ones described turn on their cameras if it weren't their typical practice to being ready to process any DNA evidence gained as soon as they got it, prioritizing it over everything else.

They'd also asked everyone to be on the lookout for a man fitting the description listed, and even had a sketch artist do some work so that they could get pictures out for these workers to have on hand, just to be sure. The captain had also made sure that everyone knew if they talked to the press about the case, they'd be finding themselves working in the filing room next to the boiler in a heartbeat and damn their plans.

It was just one more cliché that made Colin smile a little. This seemed to be the week for them. He and his partner, Derek, had been temporarily assigned to the phones to see if any legitimate tips came in that they could track down. With the help of the FBI, they had already compiled a list of likely places to be cased by their killer, but it was honestly too many for them to check out all of them.

The only thing they knew for sure, was that this man would likely kill three more times before moving on, if his previous habits were anything to go by. Colin sat at his desk, answering one call after another about the case, and mainly playing phone tag with everyone in the field. Everyone had a real job, except him and his partner, Derek, until things took off.

The two of them sat there, contemplating murder themselves as they took bogus tip after bogus tip before coming across one that might be good enough to pursue. A fast-food place, a Dairy Queen, had called in, saying they had video of a man who looked a lot like their suspect. They even had the cup he'd used to drink from. The manager had used a plastic bag to pull it from the trash.

Colin and Derek were off as soon as they got off the phone with the man and on their way to the Dairy Queen in question. They found the manager there, cool as can be, holding out the bag to them. He'd also pulled the video feed from the man's visit so that they could confirm it was the same as the others they already had.

The manager told them that the man dressed exactly as described and that he had come in and eaten a meal while watching people go in and out for a time. He hadn't been there long, but he'd spent most of the time watching the staff that worked there.

He had been quite helpful actually, already having most of what they'd needed already prepared by the time they'd gotten there. He had the cup; he had the video feed on a flash drive. He'd even taken a personal video himself just to give them something to verify with the drive. The only thing he hadn't been able to help with was the lack of fingerprints. The man had worn gloves literally the whole time he'd been there.

The pair took their booty back to the precinct, having logged their evidence and sending it down the chain to get processed. They had a starting point, and if they got lucky, a real, definitive lead on the man they had to stop.

As promised, their information had gotten processed as soon as it was in the hands of the right people, but it took time. Something similar to what they'd experienced had happened in Miami, the second city, and the pair knew that there was a DNA record of the man in the system.

They had no choice but to hand the project over to the night shift, however, as the pair ran out of time on their first day back. They got their kit together with some shared annoyance and made their way back to the locker rooms. Both had seemed to miss being able to use the facilities over the last few days and they changed into gear so that they could fight against each other.

They traded blows for another hour before they showered and made their separate ways again. They hadn't said much to each other since the bank robbery, and the distance between them had been noticeable. The two had been fairly in sync previously, and bantered back and forth regularly. They weren't fighting, but they weren't really working together either, functioning more like two separate machines doing the same job.

Colin thought about his partner as he went home, and the best thing he could figure was, that they needed to do something to take the edge off, and if Derek would not suggest anything, he had an idea. It wasn't as if he had anything to do before Friday night, anyway. Making his decision, he called his partner once he knew he'd gotten home.

"Hey, what are you up to tomorrow?" He'd forgone his typical greeting, in favor of getting to the point.

"You mean, other than going to work with you?" Derek was sarcastic by nature and Colin had grown to like the copious quantity of snark the man typically came part and parcel with. "No, I don't have any plans. Whatcha got?"

This was going better than Colin had expected. "Wanted to go out and do something. Something felt off today. I didn't care for it. Figure a night out on the town might get us back to normal so we can kick as s."

He waited a beat for the opening he'd left his partner. "You'd better get me flowers if you're gonna talk to me like that. I'm no cheap ass lay."

Colin laughed, not disappointed at all, "Really? Remind me about Carrie, your last hook-up. She got you for a couple of drinks. Why am I so different?"

Colin heard Derek snort over the phone. "She was in a class of her own. You, sir, are charity work." The class of her own was red-headed and threw a book at Derek's head as he'd left for work after their one-night stand. Colin had never asked why, but it made him smile all the same.

"Tell you what, I'll grab movie tickets for the latest Stallone flick and you can get the first round of drinks." He heard a chair creak in the background. Derek never shut up about Sylvester's movies, especially Rocky and Rambo. He had him hooked and knew it.

"I'm so in! Catch you at work tomorrow!" Colin snickered at the phone that was now dead in his hand. Derek also hated going to the movies alone, but would never ask him to go with him for some machismo reason Colin didn't know.

He settled in for the night, determined to finish the last twenty pages of his book while he messaged Christine to ask about her day, since she'd said she'd like it if he messaged her before their second date on Friday. Colin's night was smooth and calm, and he went to bed ready to sleep like the dead.

Getting up early the next morning, Colin walked into work looking forward to seeing what progress had happened overnight while he'd been sleeping. What he found was a lot more work than he'd wanted when another dead body had turned up, courtesy of their friendly neighborhood, Iceman.

Chapter 4

"Not another one..." Colin said, growling a little in his throat as he heard the news the next morning when he walked in. "That's two here, right? ID?"

"Candace Yentz, age 20. Fits the profile. Brunette, blue eyes, slim build. She worked at a coffee shop on main. They found her body last night," Derek informed him with clinical detachment. "The Vic was found with bruising on her neck and a pick of ice driven through her skull at the temple."

Colin listened to see if any new information was released, but none was forthcoming from his partner. "Did we get anything back on the DNA tests we sent in last night?"

"Yeah, actually we did, and a couple of beat cops are bringing the guy in for questioning. I don't know if it's an actual arrest, as what we have is purely circumstantial, but we know it's this guy. Just gotta crack him," Derek sounded sure, and Colin blew out a breath at the statement.

He next spoke under his breath, "As if it'll help Candace."

Derek nodded at him. "Yeah. But it should help the next one, whomever she would be."

***

The two sat just outside of the interrogation room with a glut of other officers. The FBI agents had taken over as soon as the man was in custody, and they sat in the room with the man. He looked just like he did in the videos, just wearing different clothes. He was very muscular in person.

"Mr. Verly, my name is Agent Oaker. This is my partner, Agent Hall. We are with the FBI. Do you know why you're here?"

Rather than respond, the man did nothing but shake his head, clearly not wanting to give anything away he didn't have to. He watched passively as Agent Hall took off his jacket and set it on the back of his chair across from Mr. Verly before taking the only other seat at the table. Agent Oaker remained standing.

"You were brought in for questioning regarding a case we are working on. We have evidence you have been in contact with several businesses which, shortly after your visit, produced a murder. Once here, recently, after your visit to a Dairy Queen at which we have both video and DNA evidence of your visit. The other is of you in Miami, Florida, at a Starbucks, also with video and DNA evidence. Both businesses were later found to have had an employee murdered in a very specific way."

He still didn't speak, clearly determined to hear out the officer and anything he said. He had a frown on his face, though, and no one in the room could determine what exactly it meant.

Agent Oaker continued speaking, "We also have a flight schedule which places you in Charleston, South Carolina before that, where the first of the murders took place. We know about nine of them. I think we've got enough to convince a jury, honestly."

The man, Sam Verly, sat there in silence. To the bystanders outside of the room, it looked a bit like shock, but the men in the room took it differently.

"Help us, help you, Sam. Give us the big picture and we'll see what we can do for you. After all, it isn't like you'll get anything done from here." This time it was Agent Hall who'd spoken, and he used a much softer and friendlier tone, and not a single cop didn't recognize that difference in tone from his partner. After all, what kind of officer wouldn't recognize "Good Cop, Bad Cop," when they saw it?

Sam continued to sit in silence, with the surrounding crowd observing with interest, although he did not know he had an audience, before speaking the words that every interviewer hated. "I'd like to see my lawyer, please. His contact number is in my wallet, which you confiscated."

He could almost hear Agent Oaker's teeth grind as he faced away before the man pulled several items out of a folder and spun back to his mark, "Take a look at these and see if your lawyer can help pull you out of the corner of hell we'll put you in for what you've done, then."

Each photograph he'd tossed on the table in apparent temper was a picture of a dead woman, sitting on a cold slab wearing nothing but a sheet, bruises on her neck and a hold from a puncture in her skull. The man sitting at the table looked at them, and it sent a thrill of rage up Colin's spine when he saw the marked disinterest on the man's face.

"I'd like to see my lawyer," he said again. The two agents picked up their belongings and left the room, Oaker stomping out and Hall slowly picking up his jacket and walking out calmly. Once the door was closed, the two agents stood with the crowd of officers and no one spoke until Agent Oaker said his piece.

"That went about as expected, honestly," he said to the captain, who was also there waiting. "Looking at his responses, I feel fairly confident we have the right guy. He didn't even twitch when he saw those pictures, and that isn't normal at all."

Agent Hall chimed in, "I'd say he's been interrogated before. He also didn't move when Oaker here tried to give him a jump scare at the end. He just sat there watching. Creepy."

***

An hour later, about noon, Verly's lawyer had arrived and was talking with him before acquiescing to another interview. The two now sat in a different interrogation room, and outside of it stood only three people, instead of the twenty that had been at the first one. They had low hopes for any interview that included a lawyer, especially one kept on retainer.

The only three in the room were Colin, Derek, and the captain when Agent Hill started this time. "Let's try this again Mr. Verly,"

"I'd like to start by asking if there are any formal charges being brought against my client at this time?" the lawyer interrupted.

"None, *yet*," Oaker responded with venom, "but I wouldn't hold out hope of that remaining true for very long."

"I advise you to say only what we discussed when prompted, otherwise remain silent," the lawyer said to his client. Sam nodded to his lawyer, content to listen to his instructions.

"When prompted?" Oaker said, sneering at the lawyer, "not going to just come out and tell us he's guilty of murdering ten women?"

"First, he isn't guilty until proven so, Agent." This was said with a great deal of venom of his own. The title he'd used almost sounded like an insult the way he'd used it. "Second, if you want information, you have to ask the right question, otherwise it's your loss." This man clearly had nothing but contempt for the federal agents as he spoke, "Go ahead then, ask your questions so we can ignore them."

At these words Agent Oaker balled up his fists, looking like he wanted to punch the lawyer, but he was admirably restraining himself, "I'll start us off again, then." Hall started again, trying to use his calm demeanor to ease off the tension in the room. "What were you doing at the Dairy Queen yesterday, and the Starbucks last month, Mr. Verly?"

"I was getting coffee and food, respectively, like you'd expect from a place that serves people food and drink," said Sam snidely.

"And what were you doing in Miami and Charleston? Those are quite a ways away from here." He made a small noise in his throat when he saw Sam look at his lawyer and the man shook his head.

Sam only shrugged at the Agent, before saying two simple words, "Next question."

Agent Hall held the folder this round, and he set down one picture after another, each of Sam, setting them down in front of him, as well as a copy of the DNA results, "We know you were at these locations, and we know you were the only individual we can confirm was in these cities and visiting these businesses during the killings in all of these cities." He paused, setting the pictures and data to the side before continuing to set more photographs on the table. He once again, one at a time, set down several photographs of now ten women, an extra one added from earlier.

"Amanda Stone, Leah Fain, Olga Harrow, Sara Twin, Cara Smith, Andrea While, Tina Brown, and here from Kansas City, Anya Hayes and Candace Yentz. Each one found dead shortly after you visited the workplace of one of each set of four women.

"Candace worked at the Dairy Queen we know you visited, and she appeared dead the night of your visit." He'd said it in a tone that tried to be friendly, but fell a little short at the sight of so many dead girls. "It would help us a lot if you told us what you know." He stopped talking at that, giving Sam a chance to look at the pictures.

As earlier, he appeared disinterested in most, although there was a small but noticeable tick on his cheek as he looked at the picture of Candace. He looked at his lawyer again and with another shake of his head, Sam spoke again to the agent, "Try again."

"Alright, Mr. Verly. How about you tell us about this?" He pulled out a picture of something else. Sam cocked his head at it. It looked like an old flat wooden stick of some kind, like the ones used to make popsicles for kids. It was shaped into what looked like an ice pick or something similar. "This is a mold for an ice pick, and we found this in your freezer at your home when we searched it." He pulled a copy of the warrant used to search Sam's home and slid it over to the lawyer.

Sam looked annoyed, but remained silent as his lawyer read over the paperwork for the warrant, going over the bullet points he knew should be there. Finding no fault with it, he put it down and then looked at the agent, who was holding out another sheet of paper for him to look at: it was a court order for DNA and fingerprints to verify his identity in the system.

"This one is for a cheek swab and to get your fingerprints into the system," he explained to Sam, who sat there fuming. "We have someone from forensics here who will get those from you shortly."

Sam looked at his lawyer, who nodded at him, telling him everything was legitimate. As the woman who was going to take his samples came in, Agent Hill continued, "Once everything comes back tested and such, you can expect us to formally place you under arrest. Until then, we are detaining you, and can legally do so for..." he looked at his watch as he paused to do a calculation in his head, "Another eighteen hours."

The pair of agents nodded at each other and left the forensic worker to get her sample. They walked back out to the captain and detectives, wasting no time in congratulating each other for a job well done. The three men who had been watching the scene play out all thought it was a slam dunk as well, but chose not to congratulate each other. There was still work to do, after all.

Chapter 5

"Hey, I want to go to the crime scenes. We still have those roped off, right?" Derek asked Colin.

He looked at his computer to verify some data before answering, "Yeah, we do. Remember, they've only been there for a day."

Derek blinked at Colin. "Oh, yeah. It just... feels like a lot longer, even though it's only been a day and a half since we got back. I kinda feel like it's been building for a week now."

Colin nodded at his partner. "Yeah. I feel you. I'd try to get lucky tonight if I were you. It might take the edge off of that tension." He grinned at his friend. "Could go back to that bar and give that redhead another one-night stand. You did tell me all about that 'class of her ow n.'"

Derek grimaced, "No. Never again, not gonna happen. Grab your gear. We'll discuss our options on the way to the scene."

The two made their way to the car they drove together, which luckily hadn't sustained any bullet holes the week previous, picking up their conversation on the road. "Why do you want to go to the scene, anyway?" Colin said, curious.

Derek kept his eyes on the road while he spoke. "I just have this... feeling. Like there's something we can figure out if we go from scene to scene, check out everything that happened."

"I don't know what we'll find that the CSIs didn't, but I'm game. It's better than sitting behind a desk again. I don't really know what else we're gonna do for three hours while we wait for everything to come back telling us we got the right guy."

"If we find nothing here, I want to check out the guy's house again too, yeah?"

Colin felt one of his eyebrows raise. It didn't matter, their plans didn't start until seven. "Yeah, we can go check out his house again, although I don't know what you plan to find. You saw the report on him. No job, only enough money to not work for another four or five months with what his bills likely are, and no alibi. It's a ringer."

"No, there's just... something. Trust me. Call it a gut feeling." Colin let it drop with that. He'd already agreed, anyway. He didn't have much faith in his partner's gut feelings though, since that same feeling had been to blame for his terrible record with women.

The two came up to the crime scene, a roped off alleyway between two residences. There was a small section the size of a body roped off again within the perimeter and chalk lines ran along where the body was. There were some markers still around, as the CSIs hadn't finished cleaning up and cataloguing everything yet, only managing to get the body to the morgue in the seven hours after it happened.

Typically, it only took them a few hours to process a scene and leave, but like Derek, they clearly wanted to make sure they didn't miss a single possibility. Thus far, they hadn't found everything. Derek went from the trashcan, to the chalk outline of their latest victim, to the walls of the alley, looking for things Colin wouldn't ever know.

He made noises to himself as he walked, at one moment talking himself through something and the next berating himself for being an idiot. He spent nearly forty minutes going over every inch in detail of the scene and coming up empty. Colin said nothing as he shrugged his shoulders in defeat, instead motioning to the car so they could proceed to the next scene of their first Kansas City victim.

It was much the same as the first one they'd visited, and Colin had long since stopped talking, content to let his partner live through his gut feeling before coming out of the other side, dejected at his lack of results. As expected, that was exactly what happened nearly an hour later in an alleyway that looked similar to the first stop.

Colin wordlessly drove them to the house they had a warrant for, and held no hope that there would be anything here that could help them that the police and FBI didn't already have in custody. He saw exactly what he'd been sure he'd find, that everything of value to the police had been confiscated, with one important difference.

He walked into one of the rooms to find a woman in a police officer's uniform sitting at a computer, running a program to hack into it, something he very much hadn't been expecting. He was sure that the typical policy was to take electronics back to the lab to get into them.

Colin had to ask, "Why is that here?"

He watched as the woman jumped a solid four inches in the chair, swinging around to see him. "What?"

"Don't we normally take computers back home?" He elaborated for the woman.

"Ah, ye... yes," she said, stuttering a bit over her response, "This one is a bit of a... special case." She gestured to the machine she was currently working on. "When we were emptying everything from here that we needed, someone noticed a weird electronic hitch that was set up in advance.

"As it happens, if this gets unplugged, it is set up with an internal battery that automatically runs a worm program that will wipe the hard drive," she said, sighing. "And like all good computer people, there are a couple of redundancies. It was just easier to leave it here until I can get in, then copy everything to an external hard drive."

"Ah. I don't have much of a mind for computers, so you do you," Colin replied. He really had no idea what she'd been talking about. Everyone had their strengths and computers evidently weren't his compared to her. It was interesting, though, that someone had gone through that much trouble for their computer. It was almost comical that someone was that paranoid about having their equipment stolen or removed.

The two looked through the rest of the home, not sure of exactly what they'd expected to find, but they were standing in the kitchen looking at each other when they thought they might have found it. Somehow, neither was sure how, exactly, but the earlier officers had missed something important. They'd been so set on things like cameras and computers that they had neglected more mundane forms of communication.

Rather than a phone, or another computer, or anything of that nature, it was a notebook that the two men looked in that drew their attention. They opened it up and saw line after line of times, dates, even the deaths and jobs of each of the victims, right up until the ninth victim.

There were lines of possible descriptions for 'The Iceman,' that all had a man looking similar to how Sam did, but some had different facial features. The book had been separated into three sections, one for each city, with four pages and a small stack of pictures for each girl, thoroughly investigated, as well as typical schedules, surviving family and more data than either man had expected.

As they looked at the books in joint interest and slight suspicion, they both jumped when Colin got a phone call from the precinct,

"Yeah?" Colin said, answering the work phone without wanting to hear any pleasantries.

The captain responded, "Where are you?" His tone was businesslike and brisk as he asked.

"At the house of the suspect in custody, fulfilling the warrant we took out, Derek and I found a very interesting book we are going to bring back with us. It's got a lot of information that, honestly, would be pretty hard to find unless someone was stalking people."

He could hear the depressed sigh from the other end of the line, something which bode poorly for their cause and crusade for more evidence, in Colin's experience, "Leave the book where you found it. Is Mia still there with you?"

"Mia?" Colin asked

"Yeah, the lab tech trying to crack the computer. Is she still there at the house?"

"Yes," Colin answered slowly.

"Good. Bring her back if she doesn't have a ride back on her own. Tell her to dump whatever she was doing."

"Wait," Colin paused as he arranged his thoughts, "You're telling me to abandon a perfectly good warrant?"

"Yes, I am," the captain said matter-of-factly.

"Why?" Colin had to know, and so did Derek, for that matter.

There was a noticeable couple of seconds on the line where the captain didn't answer, "Because we have the wrong guy, and we are in the middle of cutting him loose."

"The hell you say," Derek interjected in on the conversation; Colin had put the captain on speaker when he'd picked up. "We even have his stalker book to prove he's involved!"

"Yes, he's involved, but we can't keep him. Another body turned up, and the coroner put time of death during a time when we had him in custody. It can't be him. Just come back, you guys. It's about the end of your shift."

"Is there an ID on the body?" Colin couldn't help asking.

"Yeah, Judy Farrah, 19, brunette and blue eyed, same M.O. Now get your asses back here."

Colin hung up the phone, feeling annoyed. He thought he was doing an admirable job of keeping his emotions in check, right until he heard a sound from the next room over. "Got it!" was the exclamation of the lab tech.

"Fuck!" Colin yelled, slamming his hand down on the table that looked sturdy.

"What's wrong? I got in!" Mia sounded excited from the other room as she asked.

"Pack it in, Mia. We are going back to the precinct. Shut the computer down! Captain's orders!"

"Awww, but I just figured out the secret." She sounded like a child who'd had a toy taken away. She said more, but Colin couldn't catch most of it. As required, Mia was ready to go in under three minutes and the three dejected individuals climbed into the car, set to head back to the precinct and deal with the fact that they may well have wasted their whole day.

They let Mia off and went to park their car in their normal spot and walked back into their cubicles, ready to listen to messages when they watched Sam walk through, on his way to freedom. They had been sure it was him who'd done it, and there was no question he was involved, but now they had no way of figuring out how.

Colin and Derek reported to their captain to let him know they'd listened. It had become a problem since the one time they hadn't. By the time they had gotten there, their suspect was already gone, as if he'd never been. They *did* see, however, the two FBI agents sulking near the coffeepot.

The door to the room was conspicuously closed. Whatever they were talking about, they clearly weren't willing to share with the rest of the department. That suited everyone else just fine, as many of them didn't like the way the FBI handled things.

The two sat in solidarity in the locker room, each setting their work gear down and taking a shower, much as they did every day after their shift was over. Now that their only major lead was gone, there was nothing much they could think to do with their time, except maybe having a night on the town.

Colin and Derek left the precinct, getting into Derek's car. It was time to see Stallone kick some ass.

Chapter 6

As it turned out, his doctor had been right when he'd been a teen. The butter and grease would be exactly what killed him. The damned health nuts had gotten it right, although maybe not in the way they'd expected. Colin looked down at himself and watched the pool of red forming under his body as he began to fall.

He'd taken the shot through a lung and was already having trouble breathing as he slumped to his knees against the railing, failing to catch it and hold himself up as he struggled against the gurgling in his throat. The taste of copper dominated his senses as he considered his life choices up to that point.

They had made it into their seats in the newly renovated theater and had just begun to munch on their popcorn—a waste of money Colin refused to give up—and were settling into the opening credits when everything had gone wrong in a matter of seconds.

At first it had seemed like nothing, but Colin felt a familiar tingle up his spine that tended to signal danger, and his attention flicked up, ready for what he knew in his guts was coming. The shady man was wearing a pleather jacked with an attached hood, but otherwise fit the bill for a random, nondescript white man. Colin couldn't make out the face and knew that a narrow man, at six-foot-one, wearing dark clothes and a hood, would make a shitty description for a sketch artist.

The hooded man pulled his gun out. "Everyone out of their seats and stand in a line against the stairs!" He held his gun with confidence and practice, which told Colin he'd likely used it before, perhaps doing this same robbery somewhere else. Colin and Derek, his partner, looked at each other grimly, as neither had moved before the gunman and, with a nod of their heads, did as their assailant asked until their circumstances changed.

Colin took a closer look at the gun, and with some surprise, noted it was the same Glock 37, .45 caliber they used as service pistols themselves. It didn't mean anything special at the moment, but it was always worth knowing the capabilities of your attacker. Ten bullets meant their robber didn't need to be accurate. He could afford to miss a few times and still get the job done.

In the small space under the muzzle, attached to the frame, was a small flashlight. It wasn't powerful enough to blind, but Colin knew it would likely shine off of the badges that he and Derek typically kept attached to their belts, even when off-duty. They kept their badges next to their own service weapons, which remained concealed from the robber, for the moment.

"One at a time, I want you to turn out your pockets and take off your jackets, before turning out the pockets of your shirts and jeans; starting with you, lady!" The robber motioned with his gun to the woman in front, who was decked out in expensive clothes. "I want your purses placed in the bag I set in front of you, nice and slow!" He kept his gun trained in the direction of his victims while slowly taking a duffel bag Colin had barely noticed off of his back with one hand and setting it down a few feet in front of the woman.

Colin watched the woman's hands shake while she did as the robber instructed, and felt annoyance that the robber never seemed to get impatient with her, "After you've emptied your pockets into the bag,

I want you to walk slowly to the back of the theater and stay lined up." Colin focused on the speech for a second and felt a small bit of satisfaction that at least the voice was distinct and recognizable. It wasn't often you heard a cockney accent in the midwestern United States.

One by one, the line of people who had been relieved of their belongings got smaller, and the line moved forward until Colin and his partner were the only two left, as they had sat in the back of the theater. They'd watched as people gave over their things with mixed expressions: the first woman had been crying silently as she took the ring off of the fourth finger of her hand.

The next man had looked pissed off and resentful as he dropped his wallet and watch into the bag. A couple that followed looked largely indifferent as they put evidently empty wallets in the man's bag. In total, Colin counted perhaps twenty people had gone before the two of them had their turn.

Colin had been making small hand signals to Derek as they'd approached, careful not to speak as they'd waited for their chance to act. They had to make a decision about whether to attempt something while the robber was there, and they were inclined to let it happen, just to keep the people behind them safe. There wasn't a reasonable way either of them could draw their weapon fast enough to keep a casualty from happening, and their assailant hadn't been careless enough to allow them to ambush him at gunpoint.

"You don't want to rob us," Derek said slowly and calmly as the robber approached them. "You can still walk away and nothing needs to happen."

The robber snorted, "Why would I go through all the work of robbin' you to walk away?"

"I'm a police officer, and things will go a whole lot easier for everyone if you just put down the gun and walk away. Think about what you're doing." He moved slowly and calmly, so as to appear non-threatening. "It isn't too late to walk away."

"You're having a laugh at me. A cop? I don't believe it." He laughed derisively at the two off-duty detectives. "Prove it, then."

"Alright." Derek slowly began to move his arms, telling the man each action before he performed it. "I am pulling up my jacket from halfway down the zipper," He nodded at the assailant's gun. "If you shine the flashlight down a bit, you can see my badge at my hip. Remember, my hand is nowhere close to it.

The robber flashed his light down at Derek's request, and his head jerked a bit. Not enough to take him away from the moment or to give them time to react, but it was enough that they saw his reaction. "Shit. I would pick the one day a fucking bluebottle comes to a movie." The thief gritted his teeth. "Okay. I ain't leaving without the boodle, so take your other hand and unfasten your belt. Nice and slow and you can leave here alive with everyone else. Any funny business and I'll kill you, cop or not."

From outside the theater, they heard a sound and a door slam, which drew the robber's attention for a second. On something: impulse, reaction, chance... stupidity, Colin attempted to draw his weapon, taking the chance to gain the upper hand and keep them from getting robbed, when his hand slipped on the leather that held his pistol. The robber hadn't missed the action and his gun went off at the jerking motion he'd seen out of the corner of his eye.

The bullet tore through Colin's side and he looked up to the robber to see in full clarity his surprised face before he took off running. "Someone, call 9-1-1!" Derek yelled. "Tell them officer down at

Moonlight Theater, on pursuit by foot out of the theater!" He looked at Colin before running off to catch the robber, now shooter.

So here he was, after a few good years as a cop, drowning in his own blood because he'd fucked up. He'd have won the draw if not for the damned butter. The grease had made his hand slip on his holster. It was like something out of a cartoon, and if he could breathe, he'd laugh about the absurdity of it. It felt like a bomb had gone off in his body at that range and he'd quickly started getting cold from the loss of blood.

"Hurry up, Malcolm!" a woman yelled. They had run over to the duffel bag and rifled through it to find their phones to call an ambulance.

"I'm trying, damnit. My phone is off and I need it to boot up before I can dial anything!" He yelled back at whomever was trying to rush him.

"Why is your phone off?" she asked in annoyance.

"It's a movie theater. Isn't that what you're supposed to do? Hey!" the man snapped at a person staring down, lost in their shock between the robbery and the shooting. They looked up at him, as if waking from a daydream. "Go outside and get help, see if they keep a trauma kit, first aid, something! I remember reading about needing to keep pressure on the wound so he doesn't bleed out!"

The sounds around him faded a little after that as he slipped in and out of consciousness. He was able to pick up various words and sounds, but couldn't connect them to full sentences. He felt himself growing groggy and cold as the world around him grew quiet and the only things he could see were darkness and light, blurred together when a flashlight was shoved in his eyes.

He remembered falling asleep before waking up. In stark clarity, he rose and looked at the scene in front of him. He was looking down at a panicked crowd surrounding the bleeding body of a cop, whose hands were covered in butter, salt, and blood.

"Guess I bought it, then." He said as he looked down at his body with a shake of his head. "I wonder what happens now." He sat down on a chair that had been raised and felt no gravity or resistance at all, just the comfort of sitting. He didn't even need a cushion now, so long as he was like this.

He still had everything on him he'd been wearing, and as far as he knew, he didn't feel any different than he had while alive. Worth noting though, he stared down at his hands and saw the remnants of his popcorn staining his ethereal appendages.

Before he had much time to process what had really happened to him, he saw a figure enter the doorway.

Chapter 7

Patches, as Elegy called him, had been in the right place at the right time to see this man's death. He'd watched as he failed to draw his firearm and they had killed him for the attempt. His blood pooled the carpet and sank into it, likely never to come out. He began to walk over as the man's spirit left his body and saw that the stings that held the soul in place were all properly attached, just as they should be.

He peered into the man and saw the color green, predominantly, from his soul. There was a small smattering of red, as there was with nearly every soul. After all, no soul could ever be truly good or bad without a little of the other.

He could see fragments of memory as he peered further, noticing some of each of those times. Much of the green had to do with a desire to help people, to keep them safe and make sure that they'd never know what it was like to lose a loved one.

He followed that back further, and he didn't see a triggering incident like he'd expected to. This man had just decided that this was what he wanted and how he'd live his life for others. The red he'd seen was mostly limited to petty things most mortals did, small fights and arguments over mundane things that didn't really matter; like the rate at which the snacks disappeared from the break room and who had been eating which ones?

There was one moment, in particular, that was neither green, nor was it red. In it, Colin was having a conversation with whom he perceived as his mother. Patches couldn't see if it was true or not, but didn't care. His perceived father had just died.

Unfortunately, life didn't change or slow down even when tragedy happened, and Colin had needed to make a choice. He had acted as his mother had told him to, and felt selfish for doing so. He had left his home, and his newly widowed mother, to go make a life for himself through the police academy, eventually getting a job in Kansas City.

With that memory, Patches had made whatever decision he needed to, and selected a sword to sever the bonds of the soul with. The smaller of his two swords slid out of the sheath, making a sound he'd never heard anywhere else.

The blade, as it came out, was the only part of him that was polished and pristine. Every other part of him looked like it had been covered in dirt and grime for decades or longer. As it happened, that was exactly right.

He paused for a moment, as the man, Colin, finally responded to his presence with more than open shock. He looked at his body, just enough to see the medic that had arrived shake his head sadly, having lost Colin's body to the blood loss.

After that, he made a harrumphing noise in his throat, dissatisfied about something, and laughed. He laughed and laughed until, if he'd been alive, he'd have doubled over from the activity. Patches felt his sword lower to his side and he just stared, waiting, while he chewed on the stalk of bamboo ever present in his mouth.

"Well, let's get on with it then," Colin said to him when his laughter finally died down enough to allow it. "Take me to whatever afterlife I've earned."

The reaper didn't respond, only looking at Colin's earthly body and the wisps of connection rising from it. Every soul had a core, a small piece that tethered it to the body. It was that in which he had to cut. He fully pulled his short sword from the sheath and stepped forward while being watched by Colin.

He stood over Colin's deceased body and held the sword with both hands; the point aimed at Colin's chest, where the soul's core was held, and slammed it into the core, thrusting down in a deathblow. He stood there and waited for the mist that was connecting Colin's soul erupted from the body and the tethers holding him to this earth disappeared, leaving his soul free to pass.

Patches looked to the soul now floating in the air and stood, watching as the man's partner, Derek had returned, just to see he hadn't made it in time before Colin had died. He just stood there looking, his face in shock and disbelief, as he stared at his dead friend.

Patches wasted no time in moving forward with his agenda, vanishing into the dark with the soul of the detective in tow.

***

He was watching Colin as he came to, like so many other souls did, while on the boat. He looked around, trying to get his bearings as Patches pushed along the river, ferrying one of ten thousand souls he had already helped to pass on.

They stood together on the boat that propelled them onward, Patches taking in the trip's serenity as he did every time. There was something relaxing about sitting in a boat that moved rhythmically through the water, something he'd never felt in life. The water they traveled across remained calm, and the boat cut across it effortlessly in its pursuit of their destination.

They stood on the boat together for what might have been minutes, or hours, in silence. One unable to talk and the other processing his own death. That was, after all, what the river's purpose in the universe was, the chance for the soul to reflect on their death.

They eventually watched as one, then ten, and finally, further than the eyes could see, docks appeared where the boats were to be moored. Each dock had a lantern above it, and the dimly lit docks spread out further than even Patches knew.

Patches looked at his passenger, and his maw twisted a little. If he'd still been human, it would have been a smirk. Colin was staring slack-jawed at the massive palace they had arrived at. It was more than any mortal had ever seen before, and, although many wouldn't see or notice it, held details from every point in human history, and even some others alien to human civilization.

Patches had done this so many times that when they reached the dock, he pushed into it without making a noise. Their momentum arrested at the point the boat would have touched the dock and then ceased moving at all. He was the first to leave the boat, and turned back from the dock to watch his charge leave as well, who was apparently surprised at how stable the surface on the water had become, no longer swaying on the water.

The two of them started along the cobbled stone path, and not speaking to one another. If Colin were anything like many of the souls he ferried, he was probably asking himself a lot of questions about the nature of his existence and if there really was a god. It was normal, so he'd been told.

After walking for a time, they got to a large square plaza that was an open plane with more paths than he could number. The two stood at the entrance for a time before Patches looked back to Colin, verifying his presence, and then began walking off to the blue-tinted pathway he knew belonged to the young man.

Taking their first steps onto the path, Patches recalled his own experience with the path, and the life he'd relived before meeting his mistress. He knew it placed every twist and turn for each person to go through their memories, and watched Colin make his first steps along his own life's path.

As was his habit while guiding a new soul, he watched their life with them, trying to get a better handle on the man that was about to pass on. His life had been fairly quiet, to have ended as early as it did. He had wonderful parents and a quiet childhood, and had spent his high school years playing sports and excelling at his studies, though not so far above as to be noticeable.

He'd graduated High School and told his parents what he wanted to do with his life. Weeks before he'd gone to the police academy, his father had died in a drunk driving accident. He'd left to go to the academy anyway and had excelled there as well, getting to go to Kansas City. He'd been successful as a beat cop and had gotten fast-tracked to becoming a detective before getting gunned down because of a severe case of butter fingers.

Each time Patches went up a rise or down a hill, or even around a bend, he watched a scene play out in Colin's life that involved some sort of choice or conflict he'd lived through. Some were simple, others were more complex.

At the crest of every particular choice, Patches saw something flicker in his vision. It was something he hadn't ever seen happen, and it made him question himself briefly.

Feeling something shift inside of himself, he almost involuntarily pulled up his character sheet. It was almost the same as it had always been, except now there was one important development. He had new information. His soul had shifted, and he looked at his character sheet to look at the change:

Name: None "Patches"

Titles: None

Race: Panda

Class: Grim Reaper

Level: 2

Current Experience: 150/400

Stat Points Available: N/A

Strength: N/A

Agility: N/A

Constitution: N/A

Wisdom: N/A

Charisma: N/A

Soul: 50,150 Souls Harvested

Skills: N/A

Unfortunately, even with the new information, he couldn't tell any more about himself. At least he knew how much Experience he had and how many souls he'd gathered. It was something he'd wondered once or twice.

He wasn't sure what had triggered the change, though. He didn't want to assume it had anything to do with his soul count without more information, but it seemed the likely suspect.

His step didn't falter as he tried to process his changing soul, although he'd lost track of the memories of Colin. The two reached a door, similar to all the rest in this way station, and Patches opened it to reveal his mistress, Elegy.

This time she stood, and he would have defined her as ethereal, far too perfect to be a human. The closest thing he could think of was that it was like looking at a China doll based on a ballerina. Her hair was black and was so long he couldn't see where it ended from his vantage point.

She had skin so pale it could have been marble with a luster to match. She wore a black dress, tasteful and modest as one might expect at a funeral, although it was clear her upbeat attitude didn't reflect that. Her dress was worn over a body that had sparse yet defined muscle and her hands were long and fingers elegant. He thought she looked like grace given form, personally.

Her eyes went from him to his charge. She did a quick double take as he stood behind her, but it was often hard to tell when she smiled so much. She was consistently friendly, often kind and only rarely severe, except in odd moments.

"You're God?" Colin asked immediately, to which Elegy erupted in laughter.

"No, no, I am *a* god, not *the* God. Little 'g.' Let's start here: I am here to offer you your last meal. Take a seat and imagine any food and drink you want and it will be yours." Patches sat watching passively, much as he did every time he brought her a soul. It wasn't as if he could speak, anyway.

Patches watched as Colin formed a rough image in his head. Elegy tilted hers in interest and he saw something well beyond his expectations on his plate as he looked down. It looked like something found in Indian cuisine, almost. He found bread that appeared similar to naan, though it held the physical texture of something akin to a crepe, thin and full of sweet spices like cinnamon.

Inside of this pocket of delight there was meat that looked to have been cut from a standing rotisserie and covered in some sort of berry sauce mixed with cream cheese. Patches watched him bite into it, and saw his eyes open, filled with tears he likely didn't know were there. It was clearly the best thing he'd ever eaten.

A mug of beer appeared soon after, and it looked like he felt the same about the beer as he had the food. Nothing else was said as he existed only for his meal. When his plate was empty, he saw sadness cross Colin's face.

After collecting himself for a few moments, he spoke. "So, where do I go from here?"

Again, Elegy laughed, very much amused by the young man, "anywhere you like. I give you a few options and you get to choose. First, are you familiar with Valhalla?"

"Yes?" Colin said, asking as much as responding.

"That's your first option. Next is to go back as a ghost and look down on your loved ones and see to their safety and prosperity. You could also be judged by me here and now by going through the doors behind me, although no matter what you choose, you'll be judged, eventually."

She peered at him, as if staring into his very soul, like Patches had. "You have one other option: you could become one of my reapers. Serve just like Patches here," she tapped on his chest by flicking her hand backwards, "and then I send you on your way."

Patches and Elegy watched silently as Colin pondered his options. They saw his head tilt from side to side as a memory popped up. Elegy and Patches watched him tell his mother he could make a difference.

"What do I need to do to become a reaper?"

Part 3: Art Robinson

Fugitive Needs

Axis of Anarchy Publishing and Design

Chapter 1

"This is the last time." The words hung over Art's mind, days after he'd been bailed out and no longer had to sit in the holding cell. They'd come from his older brother, Jimmy. He could see the entire scene in his mind as he sat there. The cell smelled clean, which had made them better than the ones he'd sat in back home, as if they had just been washed with bleach and other chemicals that made his nose and eyes sting.

He'd looked through the bars he couldn't pass through upon Jimmy, who sat looking at him with a mixture of exasperation and sadness. There had been something else in that look, but it had escaped Art. Art had told Jimmy what had happened, but it didn't seem to matter as much as the end result to his big brother.

They had picked him up for stealing from a boss of his, blamed for stealing eighty dollars from the man's wallet. He hadn't, of course, because if he had, they'd have never found the wallet, rather than picking it up in his car. He wasn't an idiot, after all. What he was, apparently, was a scapegoat.

For the first time in years, he had held a job for longer than a couple of months and someone had taken it from him. Even if they found him innocent, *not bloody likely,* he'd thought in disgust. There was no way he could go back to that job. His boss would find some other reason to fire him or let him go. He'd watched it happen to some of his mates and knew when his head was on the block.

In his experience watching other people, dating back the twenty-five years he could remember caring, once events like this occurred in a man's life, they didn't stop. Eventually you became prey for the police and a life of crime was all that was left to you: an inescapable cycle. Now, at thirty-four years old, it appeared he was stuck in that same damned cycle.

His brother looked at him for a time, shaking his head and taking in air deeply before expelling it, "This really is the last time, Art." His face looked pained now, as he repeated his words, solidifying the statement. "I can't afford to bail you out a third time. Twice is the best I can do."

Jimmy had indeed bailed him out once before this, back in England. He had gone to the trouble of getting Art out of jail before helping him get out of the country before someone killed him off. They'd framed him for a murder. Art had been innocent of that crime too, although he'd had no way to prove it. That was not to say he wasn't a liar and a thief. He most certainly was. He was just innocent at those times.

Now, as he looked at the man he'd called brother for twenty years or more, he'd honestly lost count. He saw the brutal honesty that promised him that if he messed up even one more time; he was on his own. Not even his big brother could bail his unlucky posterior out.

"I've paid your bail, and the rest is up to you, Art." He kept his hands in the pockets of his jacket, which had no doubt been patted down and emptied out before he'd entered the holding area. He stood taller than Art by a few centimeters and had a heavier build than he did. That didn't take much, as Art was a small man.

He carried himself like a man who didn't appreciate excuses or suffer fools. For all of that, he was every bit as crooked as his brother. The big difference was he'd managed to keep his nose clean in two countries. It helped he was attractive, with a strong chiseled jaw and bright, direct blue eyes. They didn't soften much, except when it would get him something. He wasn't tall, but neither was he short.

Art kept his mouth shut as the guard opened the holding cell and he got off of the cot that had been his bed for two days. It hadn't been as uncomfortable as he'd feared. While there wasn't anything else in the room except for a toilet, it had been much, much better than he'd expected. He looked to his brother, and they shared a look that promised a conversation would happen later, when they were away from the law enforcement officers.

The two walked back through the checkpoints, stopping at one to get back Art's belongings, and the few things Jimmy had had in his pockets. Art had been in possession of his own wallet, which held fifteen dollars, and a bank card. It had one picture in it, of him and Jimmy nearly twenty years ago. They'd looked younger then, and quite probably a little happier. Life was hard after all, and neither was getting through it without some wear and tear.

He also had a cheap prepaid phone, an equally cheap watch, and a small knife. Luckily, he hadn't been holding his lock picks when they'd brought him in. At this point in time, he had seven hundred dollars in his bank. Payday had been yesterday, and nothing else but a broken-down Volkswagen. It held everything he needed to live: four sets of clothes, a blanket, some soap, a couple of tools, including a gun he'd created a secret compartment for. They hadn't impounded and destroyed his vehicle, so that was safe.

He was homeless and was trying to work his way through it. For showers, he kept a cheap gym membership. He visited every day just to get clean before work as they were open all hours of the day. It was a simple life, and he'd made one single purchase to make it easier.

He'd paid to have his windows tinted for that little bit of privacy he'd needed.

He walked out of the county jail with his brother, wanting nothing more than to lie back on the passenger seat of the car, which he'd altered to make it more comfortable as a bed than the driver's seat. The two got out of the purview of the police and got to Jimmy's car, a simple gray sedan, and drove to where Art had his car parked for the last couple of days. Finding a place to park for a couple of days had never really been a problem for him, so he was unconcerned about the state of his vehicle.

Art watched as his brother sat down and set his palm on the shifter before starting the car and speaking, "How was going straight?" Jimmy asked, curious. He had never held what one might call a 'real job' before and wanted to know. Jimmy himself was a loan shark and small-time hustler. They'd been glad to see him go when he'd come to the states, as they'd known he was crooked and couldn't catch him on anything.

It only took Art a second before deciding to be honest, and he rolled down his window and took a deep breath of air before setting his arm on the new opening as they got moving, "It was boring, doing the same thing every day." Art sighed, and he set his head against the seat back and closed his eyes before continuing wistfully while taking in the breeze. "But... It was nice. It was nice to know I had money coming every week, and I never had to look over my shoulder while it lasted." He'd hit his head against the rest behind it in time with his punctuation, but stopped and was silent, needing the words to sink i n.

Jimmy glanced at him briefly, before returning his eyes to the road and making a noise in his throat. "Hm. Sounds nice... and," He tapped his fingers on the steering wheel as he paused, knowing his next question had to be asked, "now?"

Art gave a short, punctuated laugh, his eyes not even opening as bitterness bled into his response. "Ha. Now I know there's no choice for people like me. Might as well go after the big money again. It's not like being honest got me any more. It got me less!"

Jimmy slowed down as traffic congested and took the time to look hard at his brother. "You tired?" Art knew he didn't mean in the sense that he needed a nap, but the other, bigger one.

"Always. I've been tired since we came to America. I just want to go somewhere where we can finally relax." He wouldn't have admitted this to another soul, except his family. "Not worry about the cops. Not worry about, well, anything. I'd like to live like everyone else just once." He stopped, deciding he'd said too much. He'd already talked more to his brother now than he had to anyone at his old job on any given day, and even his brother didn't need to know just how much he meant it.

Jimmy agreed, "Yeah, it would be nice," he paused for a moment, before a wry smile quirked one side of his mouth up as he picked up speed, looking at the road again. He sarcastically added, "Get that one last big score and retire, huh?"

Art expelled a short laugh again as he answered, "Heh, yeah. That one last big score every fucking movie says is out there. What's the complicated plot then, eh? We gonna steal electronics from a semi while driving? Or steal a gold shipment?" Art had no idea as he spoke just where the genuine bitterness had come from… he hadn't had it three days ago, when he'd still had hope, and a job.

Jimmy nodded as he continued to drive the two of them back through the city, looking back and forth from his brother to the road, as if coming to a decision in the silence, "I've been kicking something around my head for a bit." He stopped at an intersection and looked at his brother. "It isn't a complicated plot, but it should be good enough to start, at least for a bit."

The words took a moment to penetrate Art's mind, and as they sank in, he thought about it; thought long and hard about his answer and the repercussions it could have on his life moving forward. He shrugged to himself, jerking his shoulders as he made his decision.

He looked over to his brother and picked up a hand to gesture at him as he stopped to let Art out near his ancient beetle, "What have I got to lose? At this point, I already have to leave this state or go to jail for the one robbery I *didn't* do. Go ahead. I'll hear you out, if nothing else."

Three days later, Art ran out of a movie theater, a cop on his heels, remembering that his brother couldn't help him out this time.

Chapter 2

Art Robinson looked up from the smoking barrel of the gun to watch the idiotic cop slump to the ground, unable to hold himself up from the punch of his pistol. Without waiting for anyone else to react, he slid the firearm into his waistband and ran like the coward he was.

Oh fuck! Oh, fuck oh, fuck oh, fuck! Fuck, fuck, fuck! I just shot a cop. I just shot a damned cop! As he started to run from the scene, he couldn't get his mind to re-engage past that single point. To be fair, it was a pretty damned important point.

It honestly should have been an easy payout, like the one he'd done yesterday. That group had given him everything they had. It was even now stored in his car. In cash alone, he had more than doubled his money. Two thousand was a lot better than the five hundred he had left after gas and food for two days.

His mind raced as he ran over, through and around everyone who got in his way. He didn't even process what he was doing, or what he'd done, in his haste to escape from the officer he was dead certain was on his heels. He imagined he only had a few seconds head start and was determined to make it count.

He felt himself bounce off a big man. He couldn't move as he exited the movie theater, unable to run him over. It just wasn't possible, as the man was three times his size. He ended up rolling off of the man and stumbling to keep his balance. Succeeding in catching himself, he didn't stop, unwilling to lose time. His mind was in a panic as he pounded step after step to get away.

Art turned a corner; left, right, right, right and another left after that. He could hear the officer on his heels as he ran. Art had gained a little ground in the chase, being much lighter on his feet apparently than the plainclothes officer. He stepped up on a milk crate he'd left in front of a wooden fence in an alley and used it to vault over a wooden wall at the end of the alley he'd planned. It wasn't his first rodeo, as the American expression went.

When he landed on his feet, he found the getaway car he'd stolen for the job. It was a blue Nissan, although he couldn't remember what model. It didn't matter anyway, as it was stolen and only good enough for him to get away and to his actual car. He opened the door and started the engine, which came to life immediately.

He could feel the blood pounding in his head as he went through the process of his escape, scared to death that the officer chasing him down would put a bullet in his skull. He watched in the rearview mirror as the man behind him made it over the fence and landed well on the pavement behind him.

Just as he started forward again, Art slammed his foot on the gas pedal, feeling the tires peel out as he accelerated his way towards freedom. He saw in his mind the face of the man he'd killed. He'd looked like an honest one, and he was sorry he'd pulled the trigger. It had been a stupid reflex, but it was too late to change it now.

He was fairly certain the detective he'd shot was dead now, with how quickly he'd crumpled from the bullet, and there was absolutely nothing he could do about it... except regret. Art had a lot of regrets in his life if he were to think back, but he tended to only move forward and do the best he could. Typically, that had meant going after his next big score.

This time, in his rush and stupidity, he had run off without the gear he had walked in with. It didn't matter that he had been wearing gloves and a sweater. He knew for a fact that his DNA was on the bag, and if they ever caught him, he would definitely go to prison for life.

He thought back to his application for a visa to work in the U.S. and remembered his DNA test and felt sick. He was in their system. He'd only gotten it to expedite the process, and his brother had paid for it. Now it was going to bite him in the ass. They would know exactly who he was soon.

Art turned a corner, bringing himself down to a normal speed and matching the flow of traffic. He sat at a red light and felt like losing the lunch he'd had a couple of hours ago. He forced himself to stop his current train of thought and focus on what had to happen next. There were steps, after all. He had to follow all the steps.

He turned into a Wal-Mart parking lot, where he'd parked his car. He was well out of view of the cameras they kept near the back of the lot. He parked the Nissan next to his VW and emptied what gear he had left. Overall, there wasn't much. He had lost the opportunity to take the cash when he'd run. As he opened the door of his home, he once again felt ill, but managed to push it down through what he knew was a dwindling supply of willpower.

Fuck, I need to get out of here. The quicker the better. He sat down in the driver's seat and tried to calm his nerves and his hands without nicotine. He thought he succeeded as he started up the vehicle. He took in one deep, gasping breath after another, determined to breathe his way through his queasiness. He tried to center his mind to think again while he kept himself together.

Deciding he had no better ideas, as a getaway of this nature was beyond his meager level of preparedness, Art moved his VW away from the soon-to-be-abandoned getaway vehicle and drove a couple of miles away, parking in the lot of a grocery store whose lot was only filled about halfway. He was grateful for his tinted windows, as he knew from looking in the mirror, he was pale and ghostly. He could feel sweat on his hands as he kept them firm on the steering wheel.

While they didn't move from the mechanism, he could feel his whole body shaking, everything in his body rejecting what he'd done. Art found himself opening the car door and spewing acid from his stomach onto the street. He wasn't sure what had caused his violent upheaval. The only guess he had was that he'd just killed a man. Worse, he'd killed a police officer... in front of witnesses.

He shakily pulled a pack of cigarettes up from the center console, annoyed that it was the last pack he had in the car. His arm shook slightly as he pulled one from the pack and felt that even this last pack was nearly empty. He brought the small stick to his lips and felt even them shudder a bit as he used the car lighter to start the ticket to his mental health. Art inhaled, taking in every bit of nicotine he could and noticeably depleting his cigarette. It did not thrill him with the smokes he had bought, but they were cheaper than most, and he would make due. It was, after all, the nicotine that mattered.

Art set his head against the back of the seat, feeling his shaking subside a little as he digested the first bit of heaven-sent nicotine and menthol. He was still sweating bullets, but he'd get a handle on that given time. He took puff after puff, needing all the stress reduction he could get. When he finished it, he looked down and felt like he wanted to cry or scream. He couldn't remember finishing a smoke that quick before.

He squashed the butt down into the holder he kept in the center console and took in another breath, wanting still more air. He turned his car back on and moved two spaces over to avoid his own sick staining the ground and got out of his vehicle. He knew he'd need more cigarettes to get away from the ghosts haunting his mind.

Art had a couple of things he was good at. One important one being his ability to act naturally when he really needed to. He'd be a poor thief if he couldn't do that much. To that end, he walked into the store and went first to the alcohol section. He settled on a cheap bottle of brandy and took it to the young lady at the register. He thought she looked like a cute kid, just the right age to work a register. She was probably in college; he thought.

He took out his wallet and prepared to pay cash for his items before looking behind her at the packs of cigarettes on display behind her. "I'll take two cartons of Marlboro menthols as well." He'd decided if he was going to run, he'd at least smoke what he wanted.

"I.D. please?" the girl asked, hooking her long brown hair behind an ear as she looked at him. He felt his body jerk a little as he reached into his wallet to get out his driver's license. He hadn't wanted to do this, but his vice sang a siren song he couldn't quite deny. He could almost taste the cigarettes behind the counter and it called to him and his current needs.

He handed her the card, just able to keep his hand from shaking as he did so. What he couldn't stop was the sweat he felt on the back of his neck that had nothing to do with the summer heat. She looked from the card to him, and back to the card before handing it back with a smile. "I'll get those right away for you."

He felt the air trapped in his chest release as she turned her back to get the cartons, before catching something out of the corner of his hearing range. He could hear a radio going and tuned in to listen, "Be on the lookout for suspect, white male, one hundred forty pounds, brown hair, wearing a hooded sweatshirt and black pants and driving a blue Nissan. Suspect is armed and dangerous. Last seen fleeing from a murder scene at the Main Street movie theater."

He felt his body seize up again, knowing he hadn't gotten away yet as the girl turned back to him, holding his requested items and setting them on the table. "That'll be ninety-four twenty-seven, please," she said. He mechanically pulled out five twenties and slowly handed them to her before swiping the items off of the counter and walking out. He didn't even hear her yelling behind him, "You forgot your change, sir!"

Art walked slowly back to his car, before starting it up and feeling the sweat come back, this time covering his entire face. He ripped open one of the cartons he'd bought and tore through the packaging to get to the prize inside. Once again, as he had earlier, he placed the cigarette between his lips and lit it, taking in a deep breath, and inhaling as much as he could with it. Much like the last one, this one would be gone far too quick, he knew.

He followed that by twisting the top off of the bottle of brandy and putting the bottle to his lips. Not even taking the effort to remove his smoke before thirstily taking a drink of the depressant, he very much needed to calm down. It tasted sweet at the same time it burned his throat, before settling in his stomach and filling him with warmth.

You can do this, he said to himself in the car, taking another pull from the bottle for courage. *You can do this. One thing at a time.* Art shaking his head violently as he thought about his options and decided there was only one thing he could do... run. He took breath after breath, trying to talk himself into demonstrating courage he'd never had.

All he could do was run and start over somewhere new, and make sure that he let his brother know where he was when he got there.

He was supposed to see him in a couple of days and didn't want him to worry, as if that would be possible. Art had thought about this happening at some point, and he knew what he had to do, even if the thought terrified him.

Chapter 3

Art sat alone in his hotel room that night, in the next town to the north of Kansas City. He didn't know the name, and honestly, he didn't care. What he did care about was the hotel that let him stay without asking for his name and took cash without asking questions.

His plan had fallen to shit, and he didn't know what he could do about it. He needed skills he just... didn't have. Chief among them was courage, or overwhelming fear, to drive him to succeed. He looked at the bleach he'd poured into a bucket and thought about his gun.

It was the one he'd used to shoot the officer that day. He only knew so much about how to get rid of evidence, and the start of it was doing what he could to contaminate his fingerprints and DNA. The only way he knew how to do that was ammonia or bleach, and he couldn't remember where to get the former of those two. He wasn't going to go anywhere that night, he knew. He was as safe as he could get for the moment and he needed sleep and to take care of things.

He'd read once that it was possible to get rid of fingerprints by burning your fingertips with cigarettes or acid and knew he had to do just that to help him get away. He just had to go through with it. Art looked down at the smoking cigarette in his hand and recalled the pain that had come from the last time he'd tried to extinguish one on his hand.

He winced as he thought about what he had to do. It was either fire or acid to get rid of them, and he wasn't sure which one he'd prefer. He looked down at the bleach his gun sat in and before he could think about his actions; he shoved his fingers into the liquid. He left his palm free of the liquid, as he knew he'd need his palms to drive away, but kept his fingers in the bleach as long as he could in the attempt.

He gnashed his teeth on the smoke still in his mouth and felt his jaw clench and rip through the filter as the bleach started to burn. First a little, and then a lot, it hurt, quickly becoming overwhelming. At that point, he couldn't take it anymore and yanked his hands back out and ran to the bathroom. He nearly tripped over his own feet in his pain-drenched need to get to the sink. Deciding that wasn't good enough as he looked at it quickly, he changed his mind to the shower.

He ran to it and used his wrist to turn on the water from the spout, feeling the cold water run over his hands. In a way, it made it worse, feeling the bleach sink deeper into his skin. The cold water shocked his system, and he kept his hands underneath the downpour, hoping it would just take the pain away. He felt ill, similar to what he had earlier that day, as the pain refused to subside enough to let him function. *Stupid, stupid to use bleach!*

Art looked to the side and spit out the butt of the cigarette he was still holding in his mouth. He'd completely forgotten it was there in all the hubbub. Art felt bits and pieces of the once rolled stimulant linger on his lips, unburned and sticking to his now dry mouth. He got to his feet after a couple of minutes and looked down at his hands. To his great regret, they were red, burned, and no matter how much he wanted to, he couldn't go to the hospital for them.

Worst of all, his fingerprints were still there. He looked from his hands to the mirror as he managed to turn off the bathtub and moved to the sink. He hadn't paid attention before, but now he looked at himself and was shocked to find tears running down his face. Apparently, it had hurt so bad he'd started crying.

He was sure though, that if nothing else, he hadn't made much noise other than a couple of high-pitched noises coming out as he cried. He whimpered in front of the mirror, both in pain and then more in dejection at his failure. He had to find something; *do* something, to alter his identity. Something that worked, preferably.

He walked out of the bathroom and turned on the television, wincing as he used his burned and ruined thumb to work the controller. He didn't have a choice but to suffer through it, now that he'd made his decision. He turned on the television to find a special news bulletin:

"Police are still looking for the man who shot an officer at the movie theater in downtown Kansas City, today." They had posted a sketch of a man along with the narration and it distressed him to see it was actually a fairly good likeness of him, "The suspect was last seen by a clerk at a Hy-Vee grocery store, where he was sighted buying cigarettes and alcohol, and the witness verified this sketch, as well as giving the name of the suspect: Art Robinson."

Art felt his blood chill and that same cold sweat reappear on his neck and brow as he stared dumbly at the television. He wished suddenly that he hadn't turned it on at all. The things he saw on the television made him want to run fast and run far. As he'd already decided, though, there wasn't much he could do at night. He'd likely get pulled over for something idiotic he didn't know he'd done wrong, so he assumed.

"Any information can be delivered to your local Police Department, and verifiable and non-anonymous tips could be subject to a reward, as yet unspecified." Art looked around for what remained of his bottle of brandy and took a pull that emptied it. He needed desperately to settle himself again, and so he once again reached for his second pack of cigarettes out of the carton he'd bought. His hands were steadier now than they'd been earlier, but they shook slightly as he brought the new smoke to his lips and pulled on it when he brought his lighter up to it.

Taking in one inhalation after another, now determined to leave the cigarette in his mouth, he turned off the television and walked over to his bed, hoping to get some release from the reality that had befallen a wretch like him.

***

Art woke up early the next morning, driven from his oblivion by the sound of his cell phone. He had it set for six in the morning and decided he needed to get out before the clerk at the desk got a good look at him. He picked up the few things he'd taken in with him and walked out and directly to his car, deciding that he needed to eat if he was going to get away.

He had left what trash he had in the room, since it wasn't like they could charge him for it. Even then, it had only been the container with bleach, his empty bottle of brandy, and the remains of two packs of cigarettes that he hadn't realized he'd chain-smoked through the evening. He had changed clothes to a fresh set, but he brought the old ones with him. He wasn't burdened with enough clothes to leave any behind.

Art took his pistol, freshly bleached, and looked it over to make sure it was still functional. It was, and he set it in the secret compartment that it belonged in, just under the floorboard of the driver's seat. He'd had his brother add the false bottom to the car when he'd bought it, so that he could keep a piece near him at all times.

He started up his car, now down to eighteen-hundred dollars, and drove to the nearest fast-food restaurant he could find. He was not keen on walking into anywhere that had cameras again. He got a couple of value menu sandwiches and drove off, not thinking about it any longer.

The food that he'd realized he wanted didn't live up to his hopes and dreams for the meal, as the flavor of his escape turned whatever he ate to ash in his mouth. That, or the cigarettes he'd inhaled, flavored everything. He wasn't sure which. What mattered is that he no longer cared about what he ate, so long as he kept enough inside of him to keep going.

Art started out again, traveling west, deciding that if he was on the run anyway, he might as well do his best to make some money. After he finished his meal, he found the public library for the town he was in, threw his trash into the bin just outside of the door, and walked in, looking for the nearest target he could find. He was hoping for a local movie theater, as that was the thing he thought he knew best currently.

He sat in a cubicle in the library, looking out to the glass wall that the city had spent far more money on than they should have in the name of beautification. Outside, he saw a local park with kids playing some game with a ball he couldn't recognize. He shook his head at the sight, a small touch of envy he didn't recognize manifesting itself as a slight twitch of his cheek. He looked back down at the computer and tried again.

He searched for every version of the words, "movie theater" he could think of in the internal search engine on the computer. He found none open, as the drive-in theater had shut down ten years prior and the walk-in theater had been destroyed in a storm; still in the process of being rebuilt.

He sat back with a sigh and thought about his options while look-ing at the kids playing. He saw smiles on their face and laughter as a dog came over and tried to get the ball they were playing with. The game quickly turned from whatever it was to, 'keep away from the mutt.'

Art stood from the computer, unsure of where he wanted to go as he stared at the kids. Against his will, he felt himself flash back to his own past, playing with the kids at his group home, before everything had gone sideways in his life. He saw himself laughing and smiling, much as the kids he was looking at were doing. He'd been playing football in his own memories, and there hadn't been a dog... but for a single moment he was able to remember a time when he'd been able to laugh without care.

He raised a hand to the side of his head and put his thumb and index finger at his temples, trying to get rid of the building pressure as he turned away from the scene. Every so often, he felt feelings building he didn't have the means to process, and the only thing he could do was to choke them off, swallow them, and get going. In his adult experience, there were only three things that ever helped to get rid of a headache like this... and he was required to go outside for the one he had access to

Chapter 4

Outside of the library, Art pulled the pack of cigarettes from his bag. It was open, and he was once again shocked at how quickly he'd gone through the first three packs from the carton. He still had some left, but he couldn't think of a single time in his life he had gone through a pack a day, let alone two and change, as he had the day before.

He took one from the nearly full pack and walked over to his car, realizing he'd left his lighter in his vehicle. Art bent over the side of his ride and into it, digging around the center console for the zippo he'd had for over a decade. It was cheap, but it was something he'd gotten from his brother. He doubted Jimmy even knew he cared about the damned thing.

He flicked the striker several times, wincing with each attempt, before getting it to catch fire. Looking at the weak flame, he realized he'd have to get some butane at some point and refill it. He cupped his hand around the flickering light and pulled it to his face, praying to any deity that would listen that he didn't fuck up his hands any more than he already had with the action. He'd put bandages around his fingers that morning, determined to hide the damage he'd wrought on himself the night before.

Art pulled himself back out of the car, feeling his mind stagnate as the pressure built, but as soon as he took his first deep inhalation, he could feel some of it dissipate. He looked back at the library building as he exhaled the large quantity of smoke he'd stored in his mouth before thinking to himself that the building was far too nice for a town of only twenty thousand people.

As that feeling crept up on him, Art got the urge to destroy it. He felt the urge to take something heavy, like the gun in his car and either shoot a hole in, or throw the pistol through the glass wall and take away what was theirs... because he'd never have anything like it. He tamped it down by remembering he was on the run from the police and he wouldn't get anything out of destroying the library.

Taking another toke of his cigarette, he decided that there was only one thing to do on a day like this: leave town and drive to the next one before finding the second of three things to get rid of his pent-up emotions. Deciding on his course of action, along with the knowledge that even in the next town there wasn't anywhere decent to rob.

He slid into the driver's seat of his car and fired up the engine, looking at the gas gauge. He was reasonably sure he had enough for another day or two. He nodded to himself, finishing the last of the cigarette before shifting into reverse and pulling out of the parking lot, determined to leave the town.

***

His trip to the next town, whose name escaped him, much the same as the previous, heralded a slight change in his luck. Like the last, there was a nice downtown library where he could go to scope out what there was in the way of activity. He drove there, hearing a slight whine in the engine of his car for the first time. *Not like this, you bastard!* Art thought with irritation, *I still have nearly two thousand miles to go!*

He reigned in his rising irritation, brought on only slightly by the pressure he was feeling. He got out of the vehicle after parking and looked at the building he was going to use as his information center. This library was a large building, but it didn't have anything like a glass wall. It was solid concrete instead, with a sprawling field in front of it. Across the street was the local post office. It looked a little run down, in Art's opinion.

He walked into the library at three in the afternoon and wore the hooded sweater he'd run in the day before, wanting to keep as anonymous as he could. He looked at the desk and found a small map. "Hello!" The chipper man said, engaging him in conversation. "What can I help you find today?"

Art choked a little before responding. The man who'd talked to him had a smile that was disgustingly genuine. He'd never understood people who could be happy working behind a desk like this man was, but he shook his head for a moment and faced him.

"I need to use a computer with internet access," Art said. He was in control of himself enough that he'd done a good job of getting rid of his accent, although it irritated him to use such long words. They really didn't fit in his mouth properly.

The man in front of him responded immediately, "Alright. You just go down those steps there," he gestured down a flight of stairs three feet away, "and take your first left, down the hall. Once you get down there, you should see our computer lab. When you get there," the man took out a sheet of paper and began writing on it as he spoke, "you will need to get on computer number three."

He kept writing, looking at his computer briefly while he paused to check something, so Art assumed. Art said nothing, deciding to let the chatterbox keep talking as long as he felt compelled.

"When you get there, it will ask you for a login. Just use the information I've written down for you. It will unlock for thirty minutes. If you need more time, come and let me know and I'll clear you for more." Art felt like the man's voice was already getting on his nerves. He didn't particularly like overly optimistic people as a rule. He did nod at the man as he finished talking, though, not wanting to deal with him before he walked down the stairs.

When he reached computer number three, as he'd been instructed, Art went through the process of logging in, following the directions he'd been given. As much as it had irritated him, he couldn't deny that the directions he'd been given were accurate and concise. In less than a minute, he was logged in and he used the internet browser to find an escort to spend time with.

Art had grown up in a time and place where women walked the streets looking for Johns to work with, but over his lifetime they had migrated towards the computer age, just like everyone else had in the last twenty-five years. Where at one point he'd been able to scour a street corner, now he had to get contact information from the internet and make a phone call. It was both easier and more difficult for Art.

He got the number of a woman whose face they blurred in the photograph, but to him it didn't matter when all he needed was the rest of her. She was as white as he was, had blond hair down to what looked like a well-shaped bottom and had an appealing hourglass figure. It wasn't beyond his hopes and dreams, but he would have seen her as attractive even if he weren't desperate.

Art nodded at the clerk manning the desk after he finished getting all the contact information he needed. As he walked out of the library, he dialed the number of the escort who he had chosen and waited until the third ring before she picked up.

"Hello there," the voice that answered was deep and sultry, promising him much more than her picture and bio had. "What can I do for you?"

Art had done some math in his head before making the call, and he'd decided that it was worth the expense to deal with his own needs, even if it would eat up the little money he had, "I'd like to spend time with you, professionally," Art answered tactfully. In his experience, it was worth it to have a little tact when dealing with a worker in the world's oldest profession, although he'd have personally just said it wasn't worth the trouble to speak like an arsehole.

There was a small pause before the woman whose comical name was, 'Chastity,' responded, "And," she drew the word out with her voice, enticing him even further as if she needed to make sure he was on the hook, "how long would you like my company for?"

"I'd like your company for a half hour tonight." It was a simple conversation, and it helped get his blood going to speak with a woman who sounded like her. With the charge he was getting just listening to her speak, it made him wonder why he'd never looked into one of the many call services available. Then he shook his head and realized that the only tease he'd ever willingly pay for involved a view. "Do you have any expenses that aren't listed on your web page?"

He heard a short laugh. It sounded like silk to his ears, easy and smooth, and it excited him. "No. My website had everything listed. Where would you like to meet?"

He thought for a moment before answering. He hadn't considered a motel or a hotel. "I haven't picked a place yet. Any hotel or motels you would recommend, Chastity?" He stood rooted in place as he spoke, almost rooted in place as he spoke with the woman with a voice like melted caramel. He looked around, also noticing he was missing a cigarette from his mouth. He rectified it while he waited for her response and pulled one out.

"The Grand Motel, just off of main," she eventually said. "They have reasonable accommodations for the rate... and the bed feels good." There it was again, that tone that seemed determined to keep him on the hook. Even a dead man could get excited when a woman spoke like that.

"Seven o'clock then," Art said in response, having taken his first long drag on the new cigarette. He was personally pleased that this drag had been slightly less gluttonous than most of his over the last couple of days. It meant he was calming down just enough to get back to normal. He might just get out intact after all.

He had gone through much of what had been on the short list he'd needed to accomplish, so Art thought about it, and he only had perhaps two stops left to make before his company would arrive. He needed a fresh bottle of booze, and to check into the hotel she'd called the, 'Grand Motel.'

Art walked in, wearing the same hoodie still, when he got to the liquor store and purchased his items, doing his very best to not get caught on camera. It didn't matter if he was a little different than many of his pictures. He wanted to stay as anonymous as possible.

He had to take off the hood to look at the owner, but the man didn't stop him from checking out, allowing him to put it back up as he walked out the door and made for the motel that would be his resting place for the night. Now he had the three things he needed to get through the next couple of days without too much incident.

Art was, like the day before, quite able to pay for this hotel with cash and nothing else. He imagined he'd need to thank his company when she arrived for the suggestion. He jumped in the shower and got cleaned up to prepare for his guest.

She arrived on time, promptly at seven, and was informed by the clerk at the front counter which room was his. She walked in, looking him up and down and smiling. She looked like she appreciated how he looked. He wasn't fooled. He'd been with enough sex workers he recognized good acting.

"May I drop off my purse in the restroom and powder my nose before we get started?" she asked, that same voice as earlier coming out and making him twitch. He didn't respond verbally, only gesturing with an open hand to the bathroom in the universally accepted sign for, 'be my guest.'

She didn't linger in the bathroom, and left it wearing nothing but black lingerie, exactly as he'd hoped. In preparation, he had left the money for her visit in plain sight on the bedside table.

Chapter 5

Twenty minutes later, and Art sat on the side of the bed, breathing heavily. He hadn't said much of anything once they'd started, and he still said little now that they'd finished. It impressed him that she was as ready for him as she was. It had felt *good*.

Art pulled out his pack of cigarettes once again and took a smoke out, not caring whether they deemed alright it in this hotel room or not. He lit up as the woman named Chastity sashayed her way from the bed to the bathroom to clean herself up. He hadn't even asked about protection and had assumed she had it covered.

Looking back on his new experience, he found that the headache and pressure that had built were gone. He'd smoked, drank, and screwed his way through it and was now on the other, calmer side of the tunnel. The peace of mind alone was worth the hundred bucks he'd paid. Unfortunately for Art, there was still… something.

He still felt empty, wanting, even after he'd indulged in every vice he had. It hadn't been Chastity's fault; he knew. She was pretty enough, more than ready enough to accept him, and she'd taken part, which made her better than many of the others he'd paid for in his life. That said, it still wasn't enough for Art.

Obviously, it would be a bit before he could try again, were he so inclined, but that didn't seem to be the problem this time. The problem was something he couldn't quite identify. Something he couldn't put his blistered fingers on. On that note, he was glad she'd been happy to be on top as it made him rely less on his hands for balance.

Art looked to the bathroom door and back down to a spot between his knees as he thought to himself. He watched a long piece of ash fall from his cigarette as he pulled again on it, finding there wasn't much left. Cursing to himself, he snubbed what was left in the ashtray he'd had beside the bed. He took out another and lit it, determined to make this one last. In two days, he'd nearly smoked half of his carton already.

Hearing a toilet flush in the background, he took a drag of the new cigarette and pushed the smoke out, hoping for something, a feeling, although he couldn't quantify exactly what. If nothing else, he was hoping for some kind of plan to formulate in his mind now that he'd calmed down considerably. Instead, it felt like his mind was spinning in and around itself. He looked up to his company as she left the bathroom, unashamedly naked, "Thanks, Chastity. Your money is on the table," he said it with some fatigue clear in his voice, although his eyes never left her impressive assets.

She didn't say anything directly, but she gently swayed her hips from side to side as she walked to the table to get her money, almost as if inviting him for more of her. He found it tempted him, but he couldn't deny that as much fun as it had been, sleeping with her hadn't helped him much. It certainly wasn't worth the money when it wouldn't gain him anything, except another load off.

"Call me if you'd like to have some more fun," she said in that maddeningly smooth voice that had seduced him as much as her body had. He only nodded to her as he watched the show she put on as piece by piece she got dressed in the same clothes she had arrived in. He watched as she slid on panties, then her bra, followed by sheer hose, and then a blouse and a skirt, tucking part of the shirt into her skirt.

She put on a jacket over all of that and tossed her hair back over her shoulder teasingly.

He'd admit with no amount of shame he'd enjoyed the show immensely. It had only helped in one way, and that was to distract him from inhaling his cigarette for once. When she finished her demonstration, she picked up the small bag she'd come in with and folded the money up, placing it inside the small purse. She set a card on the table as she walked out, which he assumed had her contact info just in case he needed to call on her again.

With nothing else to distract him again, Art lost himself in his circular thoughts, again destroying the cigarette in his mouth. He walked back out to his vehicle to retrieve his newest bottle of alcohol, this time favoring a bottle of scotch. He didn't even wait until he was back in his room before he put the bottle to his lips in what he knew even then was a vain attempt at peace.

He turned on the television as he walked back into the room, this time refusing to watch the news. He swapped from cable channel to cable channel, not finding anything that interested him. He heard a buzzing noise from the table where he kept his effects. Looking down at his belongings through the haze of being mostly drunk, he picked up the phone he saw sitting there.

"Yeah?" his words slurred just a little. He could still process what happened around him, but he couldn't quite get the words to sound correct.

"What have you done?" He sobered instantly, recognizing the voice. He felt the bottle slip from his hands and fall to the floor as he thought about how to answer. What was left of his cigarette went up as he inhaled quickly, searching for the words.

"I fucked up, Jimmy." He couldn't think of anything else to say but the truth, "I didn't mean to shoot him, but..." he felt his words trail off as he sat there, scotch and ash between his legs as he sat on the side of the bed. "He went for his gun. I didn't have a choice."

Art heard a loud groan on the other side of the phone. "The problem isn't so much that you shot him, Art. It's that you killed him." He could hear very deliberate breathing from the other side of the phone call, as if his brother had to regulate his emotion through effort alone. He then heard a very long and forceful ejection of air before his brother continued, "I need you to run."

He winced, sorry and a little scared he'd failed his brother again. He didn't doubt his brother would try to help him, but he knew his options were limited. He had, after all, already told him before that it was the last time he could help him.

"I'm working on it. I just needed to pull my head out of my ass before making it out farther. Needed to work some shit out." He didn't realize that he sounded desperate as he spoke, but his words came out in a rush, not even stopping for breath between sentences. It all ran together as a jumble. "I'm leaving tomorrow. I'll get out."

"Do you remember where to go?" Jimmy asked slowly, as if he couldn't trust his younger idiot brother to understand if he didn't.

"Yeah. Fort Benton, Montana. Small town to get away to. Got it." He could almost feel his brother nod from the other end of the phone as he recounted the spot where they had planned to flee once all was said and done and they could start afresh. Nowhere would be better than a dot on the map that no one had ever heard of.

"Good. I'll be there in a couple of weeks. Just as soon as I clear up the rest of my own affairs. We can live a quieter life there, where we don't have to steal anymore, and they can't get to you. I'll call when I'm on my way…" Jimmy paused for a couple of beats, listening to his brother on the other side of the line, "Be safe, brother."

He didn't wait for a response, and hung up the line, leaving Art with nothing but his well wishes and the knowledge that eventually, they would all be in a place where no one would come to arrest them. Again, with nothing else to distract him, Art picked up the spilled bottle of scotch and took another pull. His conversation had ruined his buzz. He drifted off to sleep not much later; the alcohol helping him pass out despite the ache in his fingers.

***

The hotel had sworn that the rock he rested his head on a pillow. As it happened, they'd lied. It looked like a pillow, and when he'd punched it to make sure it was soft enough, it had even felt like it. Now, after resting on it for a few hours, Art knew there was no way in hell the thing was actually a pillow.

He woke with a crick in his neck, still dark outside. He was no longer inebriated, and was instead fully cognizant. He got up from the lumpy bed he'd lain in and looked around with bleary eyes held mostly closed by sleep crust. He wasn't sure exactly what had woken him up. He didn't need to go to the bathroom, didn't hear anything, and after looking around, nothing seemed to be hiding in the darkness.

He'd left the window open for air flow as he slept, it being late in the summer. Hotel rooms had notoriously terrible air conditioners, after all. Art rubbed his eyes, determined to get the crust out of them. He hadn't noticed it as he'd slept fairly soundly, but dawn was just beginning to break and it had begun to rain lightly, although it wasn't much more than a dense mist at the moment. He could still see the dawn breaking through.

In the dim light, he saw a bush rustle just outside of his room. It was light, but it made him jump the rest of the way out of bed and start getting dressed as quickly as he could. He didn't have proof... just a feeling; a feeling that told him to get out now. He didn't waste time grabbing much, just his pants, shirt, keys, wallet, and phone, not thinking of anything else in his rush to get what he needed to get out.

Art felt like an animal trapped in a tiny cage as he rushed around getting ready, although he had the presence of mind to slow down as he exited the room. If there were anyone there like was afraid of, it wouldn't do to let them know he was very much paying attention and ready to bolt. He walked out of his room into the cool morning air, feeling the moisture. He walked over to the bush that had been just outside of his window and looked it over, not finding anything.

He turned around to go towards his car, parked on the other side of the lot, when out of the bushes jumped a cat he hadn't known was there. He jumped what felt like ten feet out of his own skin when it ran. He hadn't seen it before. He spent a moment calming himself down and reached for his cigarettes, just to remember that he'd left his pack in the room in his haste.

Rather than go back, he shrugged to himself, confident he could at least wait until he was safely in his car before needing a cigarette when another sound came through the morning, one that sent a chill down his spine and fear into his heart: police sirens.

Chapter 6

Art ran towards his car, now again in full panic mode, when he saw the cars block off the parking lot of the motel. He had sorely miscalculated on several points when he'd chosen this venue to stay at the night before. As much as he might wish it otherwise, he knew in his heart and head there was no possible way for him to get over the curb in his tiny beetle, even if he could get it running before the cops got to him.

As the thought crossed his mind, he realized that even in his wildest dreams he didn't have the time to make a run for the car, or anything inside of it before they'd have him. His only saving grace was that the damned cat had woken him up in time to get away. He had to find another car to help him get away.

In his own mind, even as he turned to sprint away, Art felt himself wince at the thought. He had gotten lucky with the Nissan he'd stolen, in that the keys were in it. He wasn't sure he'd get that lucky again, and he hadn't ever learned how to hot-wire a car, even though Jimmy had once offered to teach him. He'd declined like an idiot.

His heart pounded in his chest as he heard car after car coming towards his position, a third one screeching to a stop at the front of the hotel. He saw both the driver's and passenger doors open and two officers got out simultaneously and started towards him, yelling instructions he was honestly too out of his mind to understand.

Art turned around the corner of the building he'd stayed at and leaped over a bush that was right in front of him, much as it had been in front of his own window. He landed on the pavement and heard a yowling cry. He'd stepped on what was likely the same cat that had scared him earlier,

"Fuck," Art said, cursing at the feline as he struggled to keep his balance as he started running again. He didn't have time to deal with the cat. He found his footing after missing that single step and was determined to open up the distance between himself and the police officers that were going to chase him on foot.

He ran across the street, not caring about traffic, running into the first alley he could. Instinctively, he knew that each turn he made and every fence he climbed over was one more obstacle the police would have to overcome, hoping to catch him. He was very confident in his ability to outrun anyone. He ducked into a third alley on his route towards freedom and, against his better judgement, looked back at the cops, finding they weren't any farther away than they'd started. It hadn't even been a minute, but it made Art quite nervous that he hadn't gained any real ground. As he ran, he could hear them consistently yelling instructions at him, but, as earlier, he couldn't process what they were saying.

He heard a click, like they were saying things into their radios as well, and soon after, as he came out of the end of the third alley, he noticed he could hear more sirens in the distance. He looked around as he pounded his feet into the pavement, hoping to find an avenue for escape. If they caught him, he knew he'd never get out of prison.

Step after step, he ran for all he was worth, as he transitioned from cement to pavement and back again as he dug his feet like so many American football coaches taught lineman to do. As he ran, he felt a strain on his lungs he wasn't used to, and he felt like it was much harder to keep and maintain enough air to run like he knew he was capable of. For that matter, he felt slower, too. It made him want a smoke, but for obvious reasons that was an impossibility at the moment.

Art had no idea how much time passed as he ran from the police, but he did notice when the dense mist he was running through became water droplets and full rain on his face. It was colder than he'd expected for rain at the end of July. The cold water on his face helped to keep him alert, and he kept his head down as much as possible as he ran, in an attempt to not have to swallow too much water.

He looked back again, unable to help himself, and saw that he'd lost ground, and little by little, the officers on foot were catching up. Art panicked at the close proximity of the officers and he spun fully, reaching into his waist to get... nothing.

At that moment, Art remembered he hadn't grabbed his gun. He had nothing to defend himself with, and the officers were coming ever closer. The next thing Art knew, he'd collided with something solid, right about at hip level, which took what little breath he had left in him.

He felt something inside of him fail and break at the impact, which made him tumble head over ass before falling to the road in front of him. He got to his feet as quickly as he could and moved forward again, only to feel his right leg give out as he put all of his weight on it.

With the water on the ground, he felt the foot slide out from under his body. At the same time, he tried to spin and regain enough speed to outrun his pursuers. Rather than do what he wanted, he felt his body spin as he fell through the air, finally seeing the police cruiser he'd literally run into for what it was. He both felt and heard a sharp *crack*. Followed by a loud *bang*. Before his entire world faded to black, taking away any pain he might have felt.

***

Surprisingly, Art woke quickly from his fall. So quickly, in fact, he felt he was faster and lighter than when he'd run from the city cop only two days ago. Normally, he would have needed to take stock of his own body, to determine his ability to function, but he seemed to rise as if he were weightless. He looked down and noticed the first of many major discrepancies in how he normally looked at himself.

The first of which was the fact that he was no longer out of breath, even though he had been running harder than any other time in his life. For that matter, he no longer felt like the smoking addict he'd been for twenty-five years as he took in a breath. He stood there in surprise: he felt like the air just moved through him, cleaner than ever before. He looked down at himself, and found that the air had indeed gone right through him, as he was nearly transparent.

He stood looking down at himself, *through* himself, looking down through his own feet, which he had thought stood firmly on the ground. They floated an inch above, and looking at them for a second, made Art look away. What he looked to were the officers who had chased him across town, still attempting to catch their breath as they stood talking with two other officers, who had exited the car that he had run into.

They stood near something laying on the ground. With a start, he felt a shock that, under normal circumstances, might have given him a heart attack. That... couldn't be him. He was tall, gaunt, over-stressed, and malnourished. He was laying partially on the sidewalk, with the majority of his body still crumpled upon the wet street. His head was mere inches away from a storm drain, limp and unmoving. Red was running in rivulets from it, washing away in the light morning rain.

He looked at his eyes, which he'd long considered his best feature, and saw the cold glassy look of death in them. In that moment, it came to him; he might just be dead. In that moment, he also noticed a thin line of... something tethering his body to the form he had now, just floating over the ground.

Finding nothing funny, he began laughing. It was too absurd. He couldn't be dead. He still had... So much he'd wanted to do, so much he'd wanted to see. The only thing stopping him from doing what he'd wanted was enough money to live on. He could have done anything then... except go home. He could never have gone home, but anything else was an option.

Art watched as a very low fog rolled in, and he watched the police as it covered most of his body. He didn't look away from what was happening, but he noticed a form coming out of the fog. Art couldn't determine what it was, but he was too busy at the moment to pay attention when the police conversation was so riveting,

"Williams, what happened?" the driver of the newer car asked. "We came to head him off and the first things we see are him looking to draw a gun and going ass-over-spleen into that storm drain."

One of the men who'd been chasing him replied, wheezing a little, "What you saw is what happened. We chased him damn near twenty blocks–" the officer took in a deep breath, "he was a quick sonofabitch, before you showed up. Didn't even see him reach for a gun until the second time he turned."

"You have your body cams on?" the passenger of the newcomers asked.

"Yeah, had 'em on since we got the call..." the last man answered, wheezing a little. "Glad we did. He was off quicker than we even got there to block him in."

The driver leaned down and put his fingers to Art's neck for a few seconds before shaking his head. "Well, call everyone. He's gone, but we need to make sure the footage goes up quickly and publicly from your cams, so everyone knows it wasn't anyone's fault. Cap will want to hear about it, too."

The officer proceeded to pat down the body of Art Robinson, finding absolutely nothing on his person except a wallet, a prepaid cell phone and a lighter. Art watched as he checked his pockets, looking for anything dangerous, before closing his eyes with a hand, as if not wanting to look at the frozen stare of death.

"We got lucky to get that call," Williams said, finally having caught his breath. "We'll have to make sure she gets paid for the tip."

Chapter 7

Patches stood there, having just come into the view of the poor soul before him. He watched silently as the jaw of the ghost of a man before him dropped, as he finally saw him for the reaper he was. He could read the disbelief and confusion on his face and knew what he was likely thinking: *Is that a panda? Why the hell is the panda wearing samurai garb? There's no damned way that fuzzy beast is the grim reaper.*

He stood, watching and waiting. Watching the soul of Art, who stood vigil over his own death while Patches chewed on the ever-present stalk of grass in his mouth. He felt his eyes narrow as he began to process the life of the man in front of him. Truthfully, it was depressing in this day and age; a very sad existence.

He saw problems one after another flash by his eyes and at one particular decision, he could do nothing but snort, part derision and part humor. As he stood there, Patches kept his left hand on the pommel of one of his swords, resting it there while he watched decision after decision and problem after problem fly by like a movie.

He felt his eyes contract again and again, trying to achieve a sum total of the man's life, but he honestly found it difficult through his childhood, through his twenties and even most of his thirties. While it was true, the pitiful soul in front of him could be described as a bad person, he had, for the most part, felt like he'd had no choice but to survive. For much of it, his way of thinking had made sense and Patches saw within his weakness a balance that rode the line of good and evil.

For all the problems he'd had, Art had gone out of his way not to harm others, other than to take their possessions. For the times where he'd tried to be an honest member of society, he had been discriminated against for either money or that he'd been an orphan. For the dishonest, he did his best to only take what he needed, typically picking targets only when he knew they could afford to lose the money.

His hand twitched from sword to sword, unable to truly decide which to use for this man, when he came to the last few days of his life: Another tip to jail for something he hadn't done, another robbery scheme, a dead detective and a chase that ended in a gutter like the one he'd been abandoned near at childhood.

Finally, coming to a decision on the man in front of him, Patches the grim reaper released his longer katana free of its sheath, listening to the grind of the metal as it was released. He looked at the thin bluish silver vapor binding the soul before him to its body. Patches strode slowly over to the body where the strand originated and lifted his sword before plunging it point-down into the heart, severing the soul's tie to its earthly body.

***

Patches stood stoically, chewing on his stalk of grass while he waited for the deceased to come around. He sat quietly in the boat that he spent so much time in, standing by without rowing. He knew now not to rush it, as the soul needed to be able to process the journey for it to matter.

While he did, he looked inside, again attempting to process his own information. As before, much of himself was hidden, except for the amount of experience. He thought back to the lessons he'd taken when he became the reaper he was today. He dedicated much of his life to learning the truths of the world around him.

Once he had finished language, he had moved on to simple math, which he was already apt at before dying. With that came the truth that everything in creation can be expressed in numbers. Oddly, some changed based on the situation, but the numbers were the reality of what each person could do at any time in any circumstance.

Every person had two sets of numbers to view: those that were current, and those that were the average total in each area. Every item, every piece of every person had their own numbers, although each being had a mean that made up who they were as a person.

The man before him had an odd description, one that made him interesting. His average total was this:

Name: Art Robinson

Titles: None

Race: Human

Class: Thief

Level: 1

Current Experience: 90/100

Stat Points Available: 0

Strength: 10

Agility: 16

Constitution: 8 - 2 = 6

Wisdom: 8

Charisma: 9

Soul: N/A

Skills: None

The numbers that made up this human were typical. Few humans ever broke past the first level and surpassed themselves anymore. Earth was, largely, without mortal conflict that could strengthen the soul.

This one, despite his flaws, had quite a bit of agility. He was flat out fast. Patches cocked his head while he chewed on the information, assuming the constitution debuff had to do with the man's smoking addiction. It was likely that it had been the primary cause of his death.

Patches looked over from his seat to the man just beginning to wake and regain himself. With that in mind, he picked up the long stick in his hand and began pushing them along the river, so that the man might begin his journey.

He watched as his guest went through the typical stages of acceptance. First, there was the actualization that yes, they were dead, as he noticed while watching the man look around to see the river Styx, barren of all but fog. As always, he rowed with measured precision, allowing the rhythmic nature of the ride to comfort the recently departed.

Even those prone to panic and fight sat on the boat quietly, always contemplating their death and coming to terms with any questions they had for themselves. The man in front of him would bemoan his death, but he would likely accept it and move on, Patches thought.

After some time passed with just the two of them in silence, Patches felt the change in the air and on the water as they moved closer toward their docking. His charge began to accept the reality and would soon be upon the next step of the process. The boat tapped lightly on the dock, stopping just as it made contact. Patches threw the noose off the boat and hooked it onto the post that would secure the craft.

The two took their time leaving, with Patches watching silently as Art decided to move forward after some internal debate. As he exited the boat, he waited, watching the fog lift from everything but the still waters behind them. Art left the dock and followed him, meekly following his lead.

Without a sound, the two began their journey forward through the steps towards accepting Art's death. They turned around bend after bend along the trail leading towards the large square, whereupon they would begin along the path that Art had made for himself with his life.

Once in the square, Patches looked backward to see Art standing stock still. The majesty of the surrounding area enthralled him. He looked upon light after light, path after path and extravagance beyond what he'd ever known in his life all around him.

Patches let him stand, taking in the view and processing, before extending a hand forward and gesturing Art forward to start his path. His gaze had been toward the end of the plaza looking at the well-kept and majestic paths. The paths consisted of cobbled stone and had lamps illuminated the way as far as their eyes could see.

They started their journey down the path and, as art witnessed his life in review, Patches looked back to see tears streaming down his face freely. As he walked, staring at his charge, he could almost see the frustration that came from recounting his life. It was unfair, difficult, and taxing on both the body and the soul.

As his tears flowed, the two came upon a door much sooner than Patches would have believed. They'd climbed nearly the entire way, a testament to how many difficult and hard choices were in Art's life. No one but Art could judge if he'd made the right call every time, but it was soon that they would find out.

Patches nodded at Art before opening one of the two enormous doors and walking inside, taking measured stride after stoic step until he came to a stop behind the figure of a woman, sitting still at the head of a large table.

Patches watched from over the shoulder of the woman, knowing exactly what Art would find long before he'd ever find it. He stood and never let his gaze drift as Art lifted his nose slightly to take in the smells of every food he'd ever loved coming from the table, and then his slightly widened eyes as he took in the woman who would give him his last rites.

The woman had copper hair and appeared to be fairly short as she stood to greet the man. Patches' view was in no way impeded by her actions as he watched. She was just shy of slim, with a full shape and average breasts, but at her stature they appeared larger. As was her habit, Elegy welcomed the new soul with a smile.

"Welcome, Art." The voice was soft and melodic, without rush and bearing compassion well beyond what Art was capable of. There was a light accent to it, perhaps Scot if Patches had to guess, but he was by no means an expert on human speech patterns. "As you guessed, you are dead."

Art flinched a little at the words. They weren't spoken with malice or glee; they weren't even spoken harshly, but there was a ring of finality and reality in them that made it looked like he would try to run. It was a moment before he approached a part of the statement, "Ow d'ye know my name?"

She laughed lightly, as if he'd said something amusing. Needless to say, Art didn't get the joke. "I know all of you, Art, and knew you the moment you died. I saw you born. I saw you grow up. I saw you leave England for a new life." She paused for a moment and her voice changed, as if in sympathy. "And I saw you die." She brightened back up after that.

"Who are you, lady?" Art asked, staring at her as if she were some foreign object he couldn't place.

Her smile stayed wide and friendly. "Call me Elegy. I'm the last one before the gate, and the one who lets you enjoy a last meal of your choosing before making the decision that you'll stand by for eternity," Elegy spread her arms wide in invitation and welcome before continuing, "Before that time comes, eat up. Your last supper awaits. Any food and drink you imagine are yours if you but will it. I will w ait."

Art appeared to take her at her word, which didn't surprise Patches. Almost all spirits and souls did just that. She sat down, unjudging, with a smile on her face, leaning back in her chair without waiting for him to start. Art's meal of choice was bangers and mash, which, from his memories, he hadn't had in years. He washed it down with ale from a pub that was also from his memories, having closed down nearly twenty years prior to his death.

When Art had decided he'd had enough, the food willed itself away from in front of him, leaving both him and the table clean of all but the mug of ale he hadn't finished. Even with the liquid courage, he didn't have the courage to ask the questions that needed asking.

Before he could sit there too long, Elegy was answering his questions, not needing his query to start, "You have three options Art," elegy held up three fingers, ticking them down as she spoke them, "You can pass on, accept judgement and find out what eternity has in store for you." Art began to quake in his seat at that option.

"You can go down and fight to your heart's content before being judged, as many do." Her voice had taken on a distinct quality, perhaps a slight edge, at this statement, but even Patches couldn't define what it meant, and he knew without a doubt Art wouldn't either.

"Your last option is to return to earth, a boundless untethered spirit. You can watch over everyone there you knew and millions you didn't have the chance to meet. Beware, Art, an eternity watching can scar the soul." His soul quivered at the warning, but he'd already made his decision, opting to head back to earth, first to watch the aftermath of his death and then to watch after the few friends he had.

In his rush of cowardice to go back down to earth, he missed the small sigh that escaped from Elegy's mouth, as he hadn't let her finish the warnings about restless spirits.

Part 4: Jimmy Stat

Still Waters

Axis of Anarchy Publishing and Design

Chapter 1

Jimmy sat in the pews; hands clasped in front of him. He'd gone down to Kansas City, where the police had done their autopsy before releasing the body of his brother for burial. He had connections, so he could help Art have a decent funeral.

It wasn't much of a service, but it was better than the cremation that had awaited him otherwise. He was the only person Art had had in the United States, and he'd have been damned before letting his little brother burn.

Ever since he could remember, he had tried in his own way to keep an eye out for his little brother, including him where he could in some of his schemes and scams, and others just doing his best to see that his brother wouldn't be someone else's patsy. In the end, that hadn't mattered, but he knew he'd done his best for the little bastard he'd loved.

Jimmy Stat was a small-time criminal. He ran pool hall scams, loan sharked, arranged small home thefts and other non-violent crimes. He almost never performed them himself, just wanting a cut of the action instead of the big prize. As a result, he'd been able to keep out of jail since coming to America fifteen years ago, and out of the slammer back home in England, where he and his brother had grown up.

At thirty-eight years old, Jimmy couldn't claim a large amount of assets, as he'd had to start over when he'd moved to the United States.

He could, at this moment, claim about two hundred thousand liquid and around fifty floating around different ventures.

He'd describe himself as comfortable. At least, he was comfortable enough to get the hell out if things ever turned sideways for him like they had for Art.

He ran his fingers through his hair in frustration and sorrow, *Fuckin' 'ell, Art. Why did ye have to kill a cop? Eight million people and you shoot the brass.* He pulled at his hair. His hair was dense, brown, and now disheveled, as his mind kept moving. *I gave you a simple job. Easy directions... Do a few jobs and move on. Then you get caught and end up back in the gutter.*

Jimmy couldn't help but laugh a little, that his little brother, who'd been called a guttersnipe, would die in a gutter halfway around the world. Almost as soon as the single, clipped laugh escaped him, did it abruptly stop, becoming anger again in a flash.

His large hand smashed down on the back of the pew he was leaning into as his anger sparked. *You were better than that; you fucking idiot. I taught you to be an excellent shot. You could have at least gone down fighting.*

His anger cooled as he looked down at the body lying peacefully in the casket. *I should have taken better care of you... brother.*

His eyes focused in on the small chapel around himself. He'd come alone, and the only people there were the ones who were required to be to make sure the viewing went smoothly. Jimmy was sad to say that there was no way to get Art back home for burial, so he'd paid for a spot at the local cemetery.

Taking care of his brother's last rites had taken a chunk of change he hadn't been happy to part with, but to him, Art deserved it. They had both had a rough life, and if nothing else, at least in death, they could be taken care of.

He gave a nod to the burly man in charge and the men present moved to take care of his brother's casket. They moved along with Jimmy to the open ground set aside for him, and the cold gray stone that didn't even carry a passage of scripture or a message.

Art hadn't cared for those things, and likely wouldn't have cared were he alive. Like Jimmy, he'd have cared more for something that he could actually use, and the dead didn't need much.

Jimmy watched as they lowered Art into the ground and covered the casket with dirt, shoveling a little at a time to fill in the whole six feet. He didn't have tears to shed at his brother's funeral. His life had taken that ability away.

Even when he was all alone, he couldn't shed a drop of water for anyone, even himself. The hardest part of his brother's death was that he had no one to blame, no one to take his anger out on.

The way his brother had died... courtesy of the body cams the officers used, the only one truly to blame was Art. *You were an idiot, brother,* Jimmy thought. He watched silently, observing his brother's burial, as they covered up the casket and filled in the dirt. It took them no more than a half an hour to bury everything that was his brother.

When they were done, all that remained of Art Robinson was a fresh burial site, and his name in stone, along with the years he'd been alive.

Jimmy took another hard look at all that had been left of his brother, before nodding to himself and turning on his heel, walking away without looking back or acknowledging the lump in his throat.

***

He drove back to Columbus, Ohio, slowly, allowing him some time to wallow in his own suffering. The last thing he had done for his brother was to bail him out of jail, not even a week before he'd ended up dead at the hands of his own stupidity and carelessness.

It had come out in the news that the woman who had reported him had collected a small fee for the trouble she'd taken in reporting a cop killer. In a way that had all but guaranteed his arrest, or, as it happened, his death.

Jimmy had looked the woman up on the internet as soon as he'd heard what had happened on the local news channels. It hadn't taken him long to track down the complete story and put much of it together for himself.

His brother had shot a cop trying to rob a movie theater, then had run. He'd picked up alcohol and smokes, abusing them far more than Jimmy could recall him ever doing before deciding that wetting his dick would help.

From there, the "escort," or whatever they called them here, notified the police of his whereabouts, and they came and tried to ambush him. He'd seen through the attempt, but hadn't the time to get to his car or weapon. He had run on foot like an idiot. No one ever got away on foot when they came in force to take you.

In the rain, he had done his best to get away before being ambushed himself, plowing bodily into a cop car that had moved to make him stop. He had, in the cop's own words, gone ass-over-spleen across the hood and cracked his skull into the nearest storm drain, dying instantly.

As far as the law was concerned, everyone now had a happy ending, all but his brother, who'd died rather than let himself be caught.

As he drove, he thought about the things he had done with his brother over the years and the good times they'd had. They had done what they'd wanted, to a point, and while he had gotten away with it because of his looks and luck, his brother had been the easy target for everyone who needed a scapegoat.

He had no choice but to go and get his brother out when he was going to be framed for a murder he didn't commit. It was their rule that no matter what they stole, no one died. It was far easier to get away with robbery than murder, no matter where you lived.

It took Jimmy the better part of the day to get back to what he called home, pulling into the warehouse completely, not willing to leave his vehicle outside where someone could do something to it. It might have been paranoia on his part, but experience had taught him it was when you didn't have paranoia that you should have prepared better.

He watched as his associates rolled up the door to the warehouse to let him in, the well-oiled rollers giving no resistance to the action. He felt the light dim slightly as the door went down behind him. Exiting the car, he stood for a moment, taking in the breath of his home. He'd converted a small portion of the warehouse to include a small kitchen and his bed, along with a small couch and his desk.

At this moment, with the thoughts of his brother's funeral in his head, and the life Art had lived, as well as his own. He was coming to his own conclusions about what he wanted moving forward. As he sat, staring at nothing, he felt like something was watching him. It tickled the back of his head with its presence.

He didn't feel anything sinister about the presence, only its proximity to him. He took slight comfort in it, actually. He wondered if his brother was watching over him. He hoped so. Jimmy walked back silently to his room, and although it was early, grabbed a beer out of his refrigerator and a snack and set them on his desk before collapsing on his back on his couch.

He felt the familiar springs welcome him home as he impacted, and he looked up at his ceiling, where he'd hung a couple of posters for when he felt like this. One was of a playboy model whose name didn't matter to him. The other was a picture of the mountains, of a place he wanted to go where life would be easier. No cops, no people he didn't want... just a better life.

After he'd had a chance to lie down for a bit, he got up and went over to his desk to sit there and enjoy his beer and the chips he'd gotten out. He felt the salt from the tortilla chips prick his tongue and he washed it down with a beer, enhanced just a little by the salt.

As soon as he got the first large swallow down, he heard a knock on his door. It was two quiet knocks, just enough to get his attention,

"Enter," he said to whomever was on the other side of the door. He still had his drink and food in front of him, and for once he didn't care if he partook in front of others. It had been a very rough day for him.

The person who entered was a woman. He'd have described her as dainty, if he didn't know she'd be willing to sell his spleen back to him with ten percent interest if she ever got it from him. She had black hair and melted chocolate eyes.

He started talking before she had gotten the door completely closed. "Hey Fence." He sounded tired, even to his own ears, and without the vital energy he tended to have. It made sense, but it irritated him that there was any difference in himself that others could sense if they were looking.

"Hey, Jimmy." Fence stood just past the door she'd closed, her hand on the back of her neck, scratching idly as she spoke, "Was the funeral nice?"

He'd expected the question from either her or their other friend, Locke. Hearing he was right didn't do him any favors, as he just stared at her. Tact was not a strong point for his friends.

"Yea, it was nice. Nice casket, nice plot of dirt to rest in." It was all he'd say on the topic, but it made him come to a decision. "Can you get Locke? I got a project for us." He had decided to move forward and damn his emotions.

Chapter 2

"A ... project?" Fence said, her hand dropping from her neck and her head cocking to the side.

Jimmy nodded once, deeply tilting his head down in the action, "Yes, a project, Fence. Grab Locke, I'll get some drinks and we'll talk about it." It was time he'd stop pissing about and waiting, he figured.

Fence sighed, puffing out a scant breath as she turned to get their associate. "Gotcha. We'll be back soon."

Jimmy had about ten minutes to prepare, he knew, and moved to get everything taken care of. He smiled to himself, cleaning off the top of his desk of all the clutter on it, setting his beer on the top of the oven as he worked. He set the chips there too, after rolling up the top of the bag.

He slid his hands across the solid wood of the desk he worked at, looking for the latches he knew were there. Finding them, he slid each of the four latches free, and with them, came the top of the desk, revealing a table a group might play tabletop board games on.

The interior that he'd unlocked had two levels to it. There were panels that slid out from the interior to extend it farther to each side, and plastered to the interior face was a large map, detailing the entire state of Ohio, from roads to cities and everything else that was important to him, personally.

Most importantly, all over the map were various colored pins and notes. Each had a name, a date, or some other piece of information scrawled on it. There were a couple of special ones he'd had in mind when he had called this meeting. On top of one of the side inserts was a stack of documents housed in a basic manila folder, which he opened and started thumbing through.

One after another, he set pieces of paper to the side, knowing the ones he was looking for. There were three of the hundred or more that he needed for this, and each other was worthless. The three had corresponding pins attached, but he couldn't recall exactly which one until he found the papers.

Finding the first after passing over nearly twenty pages, he gave a grunt in victory as he set it apart from the others and kept looking. He found the second and third in quick order, setting them aside. Jimmy took the last of them in his hand, accidentally sliding the side of his hand across the page, slicing his palm open.

He jerked a little, some of the pulpy paper pulling at the skin it had slit open. "Fuck!" He said, dropping the page and lifting his hand to his mouth, trying to keep it clean until he could bandage it, and tasted copper. That was how his friends found him when they arrived; sucking on his hand and looking over what they could at best determine as a conspiracy theorist's wall inside of a table.

"Is this the project?" asked Locke, having decided not to comment on the odd noises Jimmy was making while he looked at the board holding absurd amounts of detail. "We gonna be serial killers?"

Jimmy didn't miss the sarcasm from the man, and agreed with his attitude a little. They might be broken people, the three of them, but they weren't so broken as many of the people who kept boards that looked like his.

Jimmy glared a little at his friend, who sat there, having deadpanned his sarcasm properly for the intended effect. Locke was a slim black man who lived up to his given name. He could pick damned near any lock he worked on with little difficulty. He even had ways around many of the electronic ones that were in existence today.

He'd never met someone else quite as skilled at breaking and entering in his life. He had long fingers and tended towards jobs that let him use his skills to the best of their abilities. As far as Jimmy knew, he'd never been convicted of any robbery he'd committed, either.

That same man seemed to delight in sarcasm that both amused and frustrated Jimmy, especially now, when he was fighting the grief of his loss. He decided that the best thing he could do in this situation was to ignore the comment, rather than say something he was sure he'd regret.

"This..." He gestured at the papers, map, and pins with open hands, as if preparing to conquer it all, "–is our project." He breathed in deeply, preparing himself for the statement he hadn't completely come to terms with. "I don't want to do this anymore. I don't mind my life, but I'd like to move on, and I'd like to know if you feel the same." He looked down at his hand to make sure it wouldn't leak onto his masterpiece of a table.

Locke and Fence looked at each other before looking at him, each with a questioning look. Fence was the one to ask the question they both had for him. "Are you just sad about Art? Or do you actually feel like this is where you want to go?" It was spoken softly, but the words still hit Jimmy like a hammer, stealing away his ability to speak for a second.

He turned to look at Fence, unaware that his face had fallen and he looked like someone had punched him. He spoke before he could second-guess the decision. "I was planning this before he died. I was going to wait until he got to where we wanted to end up before making my own plans, but I was always going to fold my hand, eventually."

The two watched him, not commenting on his expression, before looking at each other again. Their look passed and Locke was the next to speak up. "I suppose it would be nice not to have to worry about the cops when I walk through a door. Will we get enough money with this project to achieve that?"

Fence spoke up before he had time to answer the first query, scratching at her temple with a finger, "Where do you want to end up? I'd like to know what the final destination is."

Jimmy blew a raspberry before answering, deciding to just be honest and get it over with, "I'd like to go to a small town and just live out my days at this point. I'd like to not have to watch my back anymore." After he felt the words leave his lips, he breathed in deeply, taking in the smell of metal and stale cigarettes from the last few years of living in this hole he called a business.

He closed his eyes and felt his hand sting before he continued, "I... don't want to be here anymore, wondering if and when shit is going to go sideways." He shrugged at the two of them and continued, allowing his eyes to connect with theirs again. "It will, someday, when we don't have enough and get desperate, reaching for something we can't grab."

Locke snorted, looking at his notoriously sticky fingers. "Speak for yourself," he said, laughing a little at Jimmy, unable to hold himself back. He looked over at Fence as she glared a little at him. "What? It's not like you weren't thinking it about me."

Jimmy just shook his head, laughing a little at the man. It started as a single breathy chuff, and became a full-bellied laughter, which Fence joined in on. It broke the mood he was starting to fall into, and when they stopped laughing at their friend, Jimmy digressed to the topic at hand.

"Alright, here's what I've got." He gestured to the manila folder he'd set aside with a hand, "I have here... a map." Jimmy paused for a second, waiting for the smart-assed comment that was likely to come. When all he got was a smirk, he continued, "Each paper in this folder has what is basically a dossier.

"Each person with a dossier in here owes us money." He watched as interest perked up in his associates at that comment, "Each document has a color associated with it, and I've kept track of where they all live as best as I could over the last couple of years." He thumbed over the three he'd taken out before setting each one down across the table, including the map.

Fence looked from the papers to Jimmy. "That's the score then? Just take what we are owed?"

Jimmy held her gaze as he answered, "If all we do is take what we are owed, we'll still be ahead nearly seven-hundred fifty thousand dollars." Rather than a response, all he heard was a slight whistle of breath passing through teeth from the surrounding two.

Fence picked up the paper of the first target on the list and looked at it. "Nathan Himmel? I remember this guy. Mousy, gambler, didn't want to lose his marriage. We loaned him a hundred thousand and threatened to break his fingers if he didn't pay up. We never got paid?"

"Right. He still makes about one-fifty a year, works for Kimble and Associates, and his pin is right there," Jimmy said, pointing at a pin that was purple and white. "He wasn't able to save his marriage, but that isn't our problem, nor is his alimony. I know he has the money, and I've even got a clue about where it's kept."

Locke picked up the next paper, continuing on their discussion. "William Darren? Sounds like a writer's name."

"Ah, yeah, he'd been overdue for a long while. I had to track him down. He's worth two-fifty to me. I took him on before you all came along, so perhaps three years?" He looked up and tilted his head from side to side before dropping it back with a shrug. "Doesn't matter."

"Why so long?" Fence asked.

"Little bastard skipped town on me. Lost track of him for a while. I finally found him when he changed his name... and yeah, Locke, actually a writer. Most of that is interest that I *will* collect."

He looked down at the last paper still sitting on the table and picked it up lightly, turning it back and forth in his hand before looking at the picture in the corner. It was a plain man of middle eastern complexion named Yensen Rafiq.

Jimmy's face soured a little as he recalled the weasel he'd loaned money to just a few weeks ago. He'd gone in with the understanding that he'd be paid back in six weeks. It had now been seven. "This one..." he tapped on the picture before setting it back down on the table. "Is the last one of the three. Yensen Rafiq. He's late."

Jimmy had questioned internally whether to take on this man's request. He'd been focused on something else and had taken him on, but for a little more interest than his normal rate of one hundred percent. If he took what they'd agreed on, this man was worth four hundred thousand dollars to him... and Jimmy knew he had it.

"I remember that guy. Didn't he get in trouble with the Italians a couple of weeks ago?" Locke asked.

"Yeah, he did. That isn't my problem. What is my problem, is that they didn't catch him and he owes me money. I have one thing on the Italians, though," Jimmy said, a small bloodthirsty smile coming to his lips. "I know where he'll be. They don't, though I'd be happy to sell him for the money I'm owed if it comes to it."

Locke and Fence looked at Jimmy for a second before deciding it wasn't worth the discussion to bring up that wild mood swing, or what it could mean for Yensen, "Let's get started with Himmel then,"

Fence said, and the three put their heads together to plan the first of their last jobs.

Chapter 3

Jimmy watched in silence as Locke did the job of his namesake, picking through the security of the cheery home in the suburbs. This home belonged to one Nathan Himmel, and Jimmy was due one hundred thousand dollars from the man for the fifty he'd loaned him. The home was a recent purchase. Jimmy understood, because Nathan had lost his original home to a very ugly divorce.

Jimmy felt for the idiot, but it had been his decision to nail the secretary he'd hired, and so the alimony was his to pay as well, as was child support. That said, he'd landed pretty well, considering the home they were about to invade. Jimmy took a deep breath of air, which held the heavy scent of rain and nature. If they weren't quick, then they'd likely leave footprints, despite their preparations.

Locke was wearing all black clothes, down to the gloves he had on. They were skin tight so as not to affect how he worked. After years of effort, the man was confident he could do this wearing hard leather gloves if he had to, although all three of them were glad it would never come to such a thing.

He held the pick he'd chosen with one hand and the tension wrench with the other. The three had already figured out that Nathan hadn't yet had time to install electronic security, and wouldn't for another week, which gave them just enough time to be on with their business. Fence and Jimmy were close to Locke as he worked, enough that they heard the tiny *click* sound that heralded their successful entry into the man's home.

Even watching Locke work, Jimmy had no desire to ever learn the fine art of lock picking himself. He'd always done whatever he could with a card or a bat, leaving the detail work to other people. It had worked out well so far in his life, and given Locke's current success, was still going strong. The three entered the house, each wearing clothes similar to Locke's.

Jimmy himself wore faded black jeans, black boots whose sole was scarred to discourage someone from deciding what brand they were. He couldn't do much about the size imprints, though. Above the jeans, he wore a simple sweatshirt, made of black cotton. The only thing that was unfortunate for him, and Fence for that matter, was that unless they wore hoods, the two of them were so pasty they practically acted as their own street lamps.

They trooped into the house, looking for anything of value they could find, splitting up to accomplish what they were after. Jimmy went to the upstairs first, determined to find the master bedroom and deal with their host before they made any noise. He got to the top of the stairs without resting a hand on the railing, before his eyes took in the shadows that made up the close doors.

He opened them, one after another, holding a small bottle and cloth in his hands, ready for whatever would happen. In the first bedroom he found, there was a small bed, the perfect size for a child, encased in what looked like a racecar. There were other age appropriate decorations all around, although the room looked as if it hadn't been lived in at all.

As he exited the room, unwilling to go through the effort of stealing the new television, he tied a small cloth around the handle of the door, letting himself and the others know he'd checked the room and found it wanting. He was sure that Fence would go over each again, as she had a better eye for goods easily sold, but old habits die hard... harder than his accent, which never seemed to completely vanish.

The next had the trappings for a girl who was slightly older than the boy, although it was empty as well. Much like the first, it looked like it came straight from a catalogue and hadn't been lived in yet. Jimmy walked into the room to find a jewelry box much like he'd expect of any female, although he held no expectation of finding anything valuable.

He found a box that had been wrapped sitting on the dresser across from the bed and picked it up and unwrapped it, finding a dainty watch inside. As he'd expected, it was fairly cheap, although it was better jewelry than many parents bought a teenager unless they were fairly wealthy. It held an inscription on the inside of the face: *For my Best Girl.*

He set it back down and exited the room without making a sound, closing the door behind him. He tied a ribbon much like the first around the door, soundlessly checking the room off of his mental list. He'd imagine that if he had looked up the information in a catalogue, each room would have run easily ten thousand, but he wasn't current on furniture prices. It wasn't his department.

He crossed the carpeted hallway to open a narrower door, finding a linen closet that was full of folded, well, linens. Directly next to that was a door that led to a sparkling bathroom. Noiselessly, Jimmy let out a breath, just laughing at how this house looked so... new and unused.

There was a door leading out of the bathroom into another room, but rather than explore it, Jimmy went back out into the hall, towards the last door in the hall, which he was dead certain was the master bedroom, which likely attached to the bathroom he'd checked.

He opened the door, making as little noise as possible, and heard the soft breathing of a man sleeping soundly. This was exactly what he'd come for. Jimmy crept into the room, sneaking up beside the bed, and peered down at the man sleeping soundly. While it would have been perhaps easier to have the man's cooperation, Jimmy would rather he never knew what had happened.

To that end, he tilted the plastic bottle in his hand and dumped the liquid liberally on the cloth in his other hand before setting the thing completely over the man's face. Immediately, Nathan woke from his sleep and struggled against the cloth covered in chloroform, but before he could really begin to fight, he inhaled too much of it to fight the effects, and fell back on the bed, unconscious.

With that, Jimmy nodded his head, happy to have accomplished at least this much of his goal. He took out his phone, set to vibrate like his associates, and called them, bringing the phone to his ear. "Nathan is out cold. No lights, but feel free to make any noise you need to. Two hours."

All he heard in response was a grunt in the affirmative, but it was enough. Honestly, they had gone over the plan about thirty times before he'd have let them leave the room, and it was paying off now.

He opened the door, which indeed, lead to the bathroom, which Jimmy found odd. He dismissed it, preferring instead to work on the home and find out if there was anything worth taking. First, he reached over to the bedside table and pulled over the watch, a much better version of the one the man had bought for his daughter, and likely worth a couple of thousand dollars.

He opened Nathan's wallet and found a driver's license that matched what he knew of the man, before pulling open the cash pocket and finding a few hundred dollars there. He ignored the vast array of cards stored in the billfold. Setting it back down on the table, Jimmy began to systematically work through the drawers, eventually finding a roll of money held tight with a couple of rubber bands.

He whistled to himself as he thumbed the cash, coming up with roughly five thousand. That was a good start to what he was owed. He continued to ransack each and every crevice in the room, coming up with a small selection of watches just as expensive as the first he'd taken.

Jimmy reached into his back pocket to get the small bag he'd brought with him then, taking every watch in the drawer. When he found nothing else of worth in the room, again ignoring the expensive television, he pulled the drawstring on the bag shut.

Jimmy padded his way out of the room, happy in the little booty he'd found, though he'd be happier if they could find everything they owed him. He thought he heard a choking sound from down the stairs and rushed down them to look around, finding a door leading to the kitchen, and then a door leading to what was likely an office.

Entering what was an office, he walked up to Locke and looked at the man. "You alright Locke?" He said, quietly looking over the man to determine why he'd made the noise.

Rather than respond verbally, Locke held his hands up towards the open door in front of himself, and to Jimmy's surprise it was a now open safe. Inside of it was a few stacks of cash and some much more expensive jewelry than previous, as well as something that made Jimmy's black little heart smile: a small stack of bond papers, payable to whomever held them with no names written on them whatsoever, each for ten thousand.

He moved Locke to the side to count them, and found fourteen sheets of paper, each written exactly the same way. With this alone, he knew their trip had been worth it and he put a hand on Locke's shoulder and squeezed, not jumping for joy as he'd wanted to.

At that moment, Fence came over, and looking into the treasure trove they'd uncovered, she could not keep the small squeal of delight from escaping her lips. Jimmy didn't even have the heart to chastise her, especially when he himself had made sure they wouldn't be disturbed.

The three stood, looking upon their booty with glee, before coming back to the moment at hand, each doing their part to secure the money they had gotten from Nathan's estate. Jimmy, taking what little jewelry was in the safe along with the cash and pulling his small drawstring bag shut, Locke taking the bonds and setting them in a safe space on his person, and Fence with her small bag of easily liquidated, semi-expensive goods.

The three looked at each other and Jimmy nodded at the other two, and they made their way out of the house while it was still the dead of night. No one in the neighborhood watch was aware of their passing.

Chapter 4

They were now at their second mark's home, a man named William Darren. Comically, he was actually a writer, as Locke had joked. The man wrote both fiction and nonfiction, although his money was handed down from a previous generation, which had let him get started without financial distress.

As far as Jimmy knew, he'd had minor difficulty in getting by, that was until the IRS had audited him and he'd been short, nearly two hundred thousand dollars in taxes over the previous fifteen years of his life. He'd come to Jimmy for the last of what he'd needed to pay them if he didn't want to go to prison for tax evasion.

Jimmy recalled the man, and had found him to be mundane in many ways; ordinary even. He'd been just a head shorter than Jimmy, putting him at just below six feet tall, in Jimmy's estimation. He had black hair that had been left to grow just a little too long, which had given the man a look like he'd been strung out just a bit.

He was slim, with little muscle, which made sense for his profession. What he did have that wasn't quite ordinary, though, were his eyes. They were heterochromatic, one blue and one green. They were piercing and, truthfully, quite distracting for Jimmy. He'd never seen someone with eyes like that in person and had a hard time not focusing on them.

His impression of the man, and of his finances and history, had pushed Jimmy to decide the man was a safe bet, since he'd found out everything he needed from the man to get his money when owed. Originally, his name had been different. It had started out as Nathaniel Biggs.

The slick bastard had gone to Las Vegas and legally changed his name a month after borrowing the money, putting him more or less beyond Jimmy's network of information. William had made a mistake in coming back so soon, though, and trying to pick up his life. Now it was time for Jimmy to collect.

To that end, he'd found out that William Darren had actually been fairly successful in Las Vegas, and although he'd changed his personal name, he hadn't changed his pen name. Jimmy had discovered that the man had come by nearly two million dollars in liquid assets in the last two years. He didn't know how much was still liquid, but he was fairly certain the two-hundred fifty thousand dollars the man owed him was here in some way.

He and his partners had successfully broken into the home, which was a pleasant home in a quiet neighborhood. It surprised Jimmy that the man didn't want to advertise his success as they moved through the home.

Jimmy had one piece of equipment on his person he hadn't had on the last job: a hammer. He fully intended to break William's hand when it was all said and done as a lesson in being a twat. He tired of chasing this little shit, even though it had been passive for the last two years. That was *well* worth a hand.

Jimmy walked quietly up the stairs of the home, secure knowing that they had successfully disarmed any and all security. He checked the doors of the home one by one and found that at this point in time, William did actually live alone, as his information had stated. Jimmy was never entirely sure until the night of a break in if his mark would get lucky and there'd be an extra person to subdue. Not this time.

He slowly opened the door to the master bedroom, letting it swing open naturally when he felt a sharp pain envelop the hand he'd used to turn the handle. His eyes flicked up to see that William was holding a bat and staring right at him.

Ignoring the pain, Jimmy clenched his fist and smiled at the man. This was not going his way. He took in a scant breath of air and struck out, trying to grab the bat with one hand while shoving the man back into his bedroom. William shoved against Jimmy violently with the bat, but found himself unable to get Jimmy off of it once he'd grabbed it

He found himself unable to keep himself from being pressed too, as he found himself forced into his own bedroom by the sheer mass that was Jimmy, "Fucker, I thought I got rid of you!" He seethed as they pair moved into the room. Jimmy smirked at the man.

It seemed even with a mask on, there was only one person who could be here to collect in this manner, "You can't get away from me when you owe me so much money, Nathaniel," he said, going back to the name he'd known was the original, rather than call the man William.

"Get off of me!" William said through clenched teeth as his attacker forced him onto his own bed.

Jimmy punched William in the stomach once he had him on the bed and he could feel the writer curl up on himself. The man definitely wasn't made to take a hit.

As Jimmy went towards his very aware victim, he took a kick in his chest that pushed him back a step. If there had been more room to gain momentum, it might have done some actual damage to him. Jimmy looked at the pitiful man he was going to maim and sighed. He'd have to be rougher, it seemed.

Jimmy took a better hold of the bat he'd taken from William and started forward again. Perhaps it wouldn't end with just a hand, after all. He went down low as William came off of his bed to attack him, bringing the bat smashing into the man's knee. Through the bat, Jimmy felt the entire assembly crumble under the force and he heard a very loud scream.

He watched as William fell forward; his knee, now unable to bear any weight. Thoughts of defense left William as his hands went away from his chest to clutch at the knee that had shattered under the tender care of the wooden bat.

Rather than work to get information out of the man, Jimmy made his move to get him to shut up and reached behind himself into the pocket where he'd kept the chloroform and rag. Pouring generously, he stuffed the cloth against the face of William and waited a few more seconds than he'd expected to watch the man pass out.

Taking the cloth away, Jimmy set towards his task, taking the hammer out of his belt loops and preparing for the grisly deed he'd already mentally committed to. It wouldn't be the first time he'd done such to a debtor.

Now dead to the world, William didn't wake from his drugged slumber and would instead wake up with one hand and one knee that didn't work. He'd likely have to find someone to dictate his next book to if he were going to maintain his lifestyle.

Jimmy felt like they needed to hurry a bit more than he'd planned, as the screams William had made were quite louder than would be expected at this hour, and an enterprising or nosy neighbor could call the police quicker than he'd like.

He ran downstairs, no longer caring about any noise they would make, and ran into his compatriots, who had continued their work despite the noise. They knew better than to waste time, and each had faith in their ability to deal with a problem.

"Found a loose board in the kitchen," said Locke quickly. "Looks like that's where he's got the money." He paused a moment, choosing his words. "How long do we have?"

"Five minutes, tops," Jimmy said, turning and going upstairs. "Get on it."

Fence called up, still holding her voice back a little, "Broken hand?"

Jimmy didn't pause as he answered her, "Knee too. Bastard fought." With that sentence, he made it to the top and without much care for small noises or subtlety, he made his way quickly through the rooms and tossed drawers and mattresses for boodle to take ownership of. It wasn't until he got back to William's room that this behavior bore fruit.

When he tossed William's bed, he found a small stash of cash underneath the mattress, but he also noticed a small tear in the fabric that had been obviously mended. Rather than waste the time reaching for a tool, Jimmy used his hands to peel apart the mattress to find a stash of cash that, at first glance, looked to be about ten thousand, maybe more.

He took it into his custody and made his way through the drawers and the wallet of William, finding nothing more of any interest. Job done, he left the upstairs to find he was the last one to finish, and the three made their way out of the home with celerity.

Back in their humble abode, Jimmy, Locke, and Fence spilled out their haul on the table in the back after each had deposited their clothes at the laundry and switched into things they were more comfortable in to count everything in front of themselves. Each set to work on their respective piles, thumbing through everything.

Fence had the most interesting pile, as she had the previous time. Setting aside numerous trinkets and basic jewelry, the worth of which she understood better than anybody else. On the first job, she'd sold her section for a neat seven thousand dollars, on top of everything else they had. He had no idea what she thought she could fetch for the items she had in front of her at the moment, but he couldn't wait to find out.

He thumbed each bill with a delicate finger, letting his thumb pass over the ripples and texture lovingly. It really was his favorite part of the job; counting money. He had gotten away from it recently with everything that had happened, but it brought his heart joy to count his gains. He took longer to count than either Locke or Fence, taking joy with every bill he set aside.

As the other two watched, he began to hum to himself as he started counting out loud, "One hundred more... three thousand two hundred... three thousand three hundred... hahaha. Oh thank you William, Four thousand..."

"Should we leave you alone with those?" Fence said, uncharacteristically going for the comment before Locke could.

Jimmy didn't respond with words, only laughing for a moment before maintaining his focus on the count. "Seven thousand... ha ha ha..."

Ten minutes later, and a quick break for Locke and Fence, he had finally finished counting. What they hadn't expected was the single tear that rolled down his face as he got to the end of his portion. "Boss?" Locke said, unsure of how to ask what he wanted.

"This... this would have been enough to get Art out... and we aren't even done yet." The joy he'd had on his face was gone now, replaced with misery he had trouble bottling up. He felt anger, sadness, and something in the pit of his stomach he didn't recognize, except it felt akin to being sick in one way or another.

He tasted saltwater on his tongue as he stuck it out to lick at the odd feeling on his cheek and immediately reached a hand up to feel the tear that had rolled down. It had been so long since he'd cried even this much that it didn't even occur to him to hide it. He felt his eyes widen as he held them out to get a better look at his first tear in over fifteen years.

He stared for a few seconds at the finger that glistened under the light of the room before feeling his hand clench in front of him when his anger surfaced again. Impotent anger and pain took over him and he didn't notice at all when the other two left him alone with his emotions.

They didn't see when he bit down on his own fist and they didn't hear when he yelled at it before turning and punching the concrete wall behind himself. He had just enough control to keep from smashing his hand into the table he'd probably crack, but not enough to keep from hearing the *click* of his wrist dislocating at the punch that hadn't been straight on.

In his grief, he didn't feel as much of the pain as he should have and only held the wrist with his other hand, rotating it until it fell back into place.

Later, he'd found out it would hurt for a fairly long while before it would feel normal again. Coming back to the moment, he sat, rotating the wrist as he looked at the money and the map, thinking to himself, *Only one more to go, Art. Then I'll live the life we both wanted in peace.*

Chapter 5

Fuck me, Jimmy thought to himself as he swung from the rafters. Everything had gone according to plan. Every single thing had gone right. Up until, it hadn't. The job was supposed to have been easy, and on paper it had been an immaculate masterpiece. Reality is never so kind.

Jimmy, Locke, and Fence had spent days on this job, even going so far as to scope out the premises for a week before committing. They'd taken a single black sedan out of Columbus on their search for Yensen's stash, before coming to the small home they were dead certain he was staying in. He'd never admit it to himself or anyone else, but he was actually quite jealous of what looked like a nice, quiet home.

He knew in that home lay the rest of the money he was owed, as Yensen was most assuredly too paranoid to trust his money to a bank, given the connections he had. Yensen's money, along with the rest he and his merry troupe had liberated, would set them up for a few years, if not the rest of their life, if they were frugal.

They had filled the economy car with all the gear they thought they would need, even going farther in preparation than their other jobs. Along with the typical black garb they wore and the personal tools each used, they had full sets of climbing gear and ropes in the car, as well as odd tools like a butane torch and even a sander if one of them got stupid and left a print. They couldn't get rid of the print from the finger, but they could sure as hell sand down the area they'd laid it.

They had decided to make the drive at an hour past midnight, two hours earlier than needed, just to make sure they had the time to get everything from their mark. They rolled up to the home, a brown that bordered on black in the dim of twilight, with white trim that stood stark in the moonlight.

Although they didn't have to be quiet yet, each was silent, contemplating their part in this. Jimmy tasted the cigarette he'd snuffed out ten minutes ago, the ash never quite leaving his tongue. Locke sat fiddling with his lock picks while Fence had in a single ear bud, listening to some kind of music to keep relaxed.

Checking the timepiece he rarely wore, Jimmy nodded back at his crew. "Time to go to work, Locke." He watched as his friend nodded at him and slipped from the car into the night like a ghost. He tried to keep track of the man, but only saw a ripple of movement every couple of seconds as he moved to the window they'd designated as their entry. Yensen had no smart devices or electronic locks. Clearly afraid of showing up on someone's radar, Jimmy guessed.

Against the window, Jimmy could barely make out the form of Locke as he worked his magic on the looking glass, taking experience and logic to follow the man's actions. He felt a slight buzz in his hand as the movement stopped at the window and gazed down at the message telling them to go for it. On his way out, Jimmy paid too much attention to the form of Locke he was still attempting to make out, and smashed his head into the door frame, not making a sound as he silently cursed the car.

He finally got a look at the full form of Locke as he sat there with a paper-thin sheet of metal pushed through the frame of the window, ready to pop the latch. At a nod from both Jimmy and Fence, he pushed in, causing the lock to release silently.

Locke swapped his tool for a small pry bar and levered the window up to an open position. It was well-enough cared for that it made no sound as it rose, and stayed in place as force left it in place.

Moments later, the three of them climbing through the breach, Locke going first to check for their landing site, and moving a few small items to the side before moving the table that had been placed under the windowsill. He'd joked that he was confident in himself and his breaking and entering, but he didn't trust Jimmy or Fence not to fuck up his perfect record.

Before he'd let them in the home, Locke waggled a finger at the two interlopers he'd come with and gestured at their feet, unwilling to give on the point he'd made earlier: that shoes made too much damned noise and clothes companies made socks that didn't slide that were worth twice their weight in gold when trying to maintain stealth.

After following Locke's unspoken orders, the trio separated as they normally did, Locke and Fence breaking off into what they'd figured was the kitchen while sorting through drawers and looking for any rooms that were hidden.

Jimmy did as normal and went up the stairs to silence any people in the household. He knew there should be at least one, as there was a car in the driveway that belonged to a member of the home.

Jimmy walked up the stairs, looking both left and right when he got to the top. He took in a breath, smelling the air. If he had to pick what to call it, he'd say it smelled *too* clean. Like someone had doused it in chemicals to get rid of anything lingering, which was a bit odd. He walked down the right side of the hall, seeing that everything looked as if it belonged in a showroom, as opposed to being lived in.

He opened the first door and saw that other than a bed with clean sheets; the room was not furnished at all. Turning on a heel and trying to ignore the feeling he felt creeping up on him, he quietly stalked across the hall to the next room. It was a mirror image of the first, with nothing but a queen bed with sheets and the smell and feel of somewhere untouched by humanity.

He picked up his pace as he made his way back across to the other side. He hadn't worked yet to come up to a single door, presumably the master bedroom. He opened the door silently, looking for anyone that would need to be put to sleep and found, once again, a room he was almost terrified of. It wasn't supposed to be an empty home.

He found a room that had a larger bed, with a small empty chest that had an open lid and nothing else again. Rather than stand to dwell on what he was looking at, he started to move even faster, with almost no stealth as he hurried down the stairs.

He came down to find his two companions standing at the foot of the stairs, waiting for him, looking likely as spooked as he felt. Something was definitely wrong. He looked over to the kitchen the two had gone through to find that it was much like every room he'd been in. There were three stools at the bar and what looked like an untouched kitchen.

There was only one place the trio hadn't looked at inside the home, and it was the only thing that didn't look untouched. There was a door at the corner of the kitchen space that, they assumed, led to a basement or cellar for preserved foods they were going to explore. Jimmy, despite his apprehension, wasn't willing to let this go without exploring every nook and cranny available to him.

They opened the door slowly, and unlike the rest of the home, this didn't look wiped down with a toothbrush. They found the expected things: a washer, a dryer, a television and a beat-up couch facing it.

They took the well-maintained steps down and looked around after flipping the light switch to the "on" position.

All around the basement were studs, unfinished walls that looked as if they could have used insulation and drywall to make the room look like the rest of the house. In some studs were electrical wiring, leading to outlets, some of which had devices plugged in, like the television.

The one part of the room that they found bizarre was that the someone had pulled the washer and dryer back from the wall, much farther than they normally should have been. Behind them, Jimmy saw what looked like a small safe that had been hidden in the wall behind the two appliances. Unfortunately, like the rest of the home, it was completely empty and devoid of any contents. Whatever had been here… no longer was.

To Jimmy, the last message he'd needed had been delivered as a crimson flag, telling him to get the hell out as soon as possible. He quickly spun to his two companions, and they decided as a group that they needed to leave. Now.

The trio abandoned their stealth and rushed out of the basement, only taking enough time to make sure that they would not trip over anything or leave marks they didn't mean to on any of the surfaces of the creepily immaculate home.

As they got to the top, Locke, who was first in their line, crashed through the door of the basement and didn't even bother to look back at his friends, trusting that they'd be up shortly. He quickly vanished from view as they ran up the stairs.

Fence was next, turning the corner at the top of the stairs and vanishing from Jimmy's sight. As he got to the top himself, he spun to the side to make his way through the home and back out the window they'd entered from. Rather than do as he wished, he felt his world go completely black as something was pulled over his skull and he surrendered to darkness as a jolt ran through his body.

Chapter 6

Jimmy came to, finding himself slowly rotating in a circle as he hung from something. He didn't open his eyes yet, and focused on how his body felt, taking in a shuddering breath deep inside. He smelled iron and shook at the pain the action elicited from him.

He felt like something very coarse was digging into his wrists, but with how they felt he couldn't do anything, so instead kept focusing on the rest of his body.

He flexed his muscles, finding many of them in pain, as if a rolling pin had tenderized him. Cracking open his eyes, he looked down to find much of his visible body purple and black.

Looking up to his wrists, Jimmy find blood oozing down his arms as the rope holding him up had cut right through the skin. The rope holding him was hanging from a meat hook and his feet were very much off of the ground, meaning his whole body was being supported by his bound wrists.

Slowly, he turned his head to each side, finding his companions on either side of him. "Good morning," said a voice in a distinctly French accent, which he pegged as odd, considering it was the Italians who wanted Yensen. "You're going to answer some questions for me."

He spun the chains holding Jimmy up to make sure he could see the condition of his two companions. They'd been stripped down to a shirt and jeans, both of which were in poor shape.

He drew in a breath at the sight and jolted in his restraints at the pain. He felt everything that he had noticed earlier again, sharper, as he'd breathed in too quickly at seeing his friends in a condition much like his own. It almost felt like his body was being torn apart, because literally all of him hurt.

"Now that I have your 'undivided' attention, you can answer a few questions for me. Where has Yensen gone?" The man's voice was clear, concise, and nearly pleasant as he spoke to the trio, but Jimmy had no delusions about the threat and the danger of the man who spoke.

The speaker appeared well-mannered, speaking in a cultured tone that fit what he wore and how he sat. He was sitting on a stool, looking at the three pitiful intruders that he'd caught with a strange expression on his face. It was a mixture of boredom and... glee? Jimmy couldn't tell what it meant at first, but he had an idea from their situation.

This unknown was thin, well maintained and wearing a suit that was obviously tailored to fit his body perfectly. It might have been Armani, but Jimmy didn't have an eye for fashion, tending to cheap and serviceable. As he turned with the rope, Jimmy got a look at hands neatly folded over a knee that was folded properly over his other leg while the man sat back.

If he were standing, the man might have been over six-feet tall, but he couldn't tell. He was clean shaven, and his hair was slicked back with what was likely expensive product, letting the neatly trimmed black and gray strands shine.

It was the eyes that really tipped Jimmy off they were in much deeper than any of them had wanted. They promised a willingness to do anything for what this man wanted. That said, unfortunately, he likely didn't have what this man wanted.

"We... dunno, mate," He replied, his accent coming out more with the pain. "We came to... 'is 'ouse to collect a debt." Jimmy had no intention of protecting Yensen, but he was afraid none of his people knew the answers this man was looking for. There was nothing he or either of his friends, who both stayed silent, could do to save themselves from whatever this man would do to them, and Jimmy knew it.

He watched in horror as the man nodded at another who was holding a rusted set of pliers, and he walked over to Locke, who looked more purple than black. Locke's face visibly paled as the man came closer before cuffing his foot to keep it in place. Jimmy's stomach turned, and he looked away at the screams that ensued as Locke's largest toenail was ripped out.

As the screams subsided, Jimmy could hear Fence retch and cough up acid. He'd barely manage to keep from doing the same himself. He was not cut out for this level of crime, and the torture he was about to endure made that painfully clear to him. The man nodded to his men again, and they took buckets of water and threw them on Jimmy, Fence, and Locke, ensuring their continued attention.

"I know you can do better than that. Tell me where he would go, and I could be convinced to let your friends go. Otherwise, I can be quite creative." Jimmy felt his blood go cold at the thought. This man had only started, and what he'd done was more than anyone in his crew could take. He knew there were much more creative ways to get people to talk.

Before Jimmy could answer with the truth, that he didn't know where Yensen had gone, the man continued, "I must admit... I do love the old ways the best, though. Let's see if your friend knows more than you before we get to you."

He watched, and felt the acid in his stomach boil up as a man came out from another room with a small pot, a rat, and some hot coals. What was about to happen was simple. The pot was going to get tied to Locke's stomach and the red-hot coals would heat the pot until the rat had no way to escape... other than through Locke.

"Tell me what I want to know. Where is Yensen?" Jimmy watched as Locke thrashed in his chains, trying to dislodge the pot before it could heat up. Jimmy felt like it took hours and he began to smell the heat rising from it. Locke cried out as the first scratches set in and the man questioning them repeated himself, "Where is Yensen?"

Locke began to scream and cry as his situation escalated, before the pain caused him to pass out, never to wake again as the rat burrowed through his insides. Their captors didn't turn away until they saw a liberal quantity of blood run down his legs. They then turned their attention to Fence.

Much to Jimmy's terror, the man hadn't even flinched at the barbaric way he'd killed Locke, and even seemed to enjoy the spectacle of watching a rat tear its way through the guts of another human being. They could smell the stink coming from Locke, as his bowels had evacuated in his death. It made sense as Jimmy imagined they'd been out cold for a few hours.

"Next is you, my dear. Tell me, where has Yensen gone?" Fence was crying openly, having watched in horror, unable to look away, as Locke was bleeding openly down his pants as he swung limply. He motioned to his men, who walked out and back in with red pokers and a bucket of coals. He smiled as he looked at her, calmly asking the same again in a voice of absolute peace.

She couldn't stop herself from crying long enough to breathe to answer the questions, and screamed as the first poker was laid against her bare feet, burning her as it was held there. "I don't like torturing women," the man said. "but I will tell you right now that it will be worse for you than anyone else in what I am willing to do to get answers." Unfortunately, whomever this man was, he was every bit as good as his word.

What happened to Fence took more than an hour, and Jimmy was grateful to be a man when he saw just what their captor had been willing to do to procure his information from Fence. It had been... grotesque and perverse on a level Jimmy had never heard of, much less expected to experience. He looked at Fence and couldn't muster the voice to talk. He could only look at her in pity: beaten, broken, and used in ways that had made him heave for the entire duration at how they had defiled her.

Turning to Jimmy, their captor smiled in a way that chilled him to the bone. They'd already told him everything they knew of Yensen, before even Locke had met his end. It hadn't even been anything that they'd wanted or cared to hear and at this point, Jimmy was sure they'd kill him in some gruesome fashion just to do it.

He saw nothing but a knife in the hand of a minion of their captor, although that was nothing to be excited about, as he was just now realizing what they could do to a person before they actually died. He screamed as the knife drew a line down his arm, trying to twist away and unable to do so. Hearing it, he knew his scream was more terror than pain and he didn't want to know just what was going to happen to him as he heard the dreaded question again.

"Where is Yensen?" He felt the blade come down again along roughly the same path, coming to a single point where the first line had ended. He didn't respond to the pleasantly asked question, but instead kept yelling in his futile attempt to get away. Fence had done the same as he did, as had Locke. Neither managed to do anything more than prolong their ordeal.

The man cutting him flicked the knife under the point, lifting away a small piece of his skin. His scream changed pitch at the horrific realization of what they had planned for him and he didn't even notice the catch in his breath or the tears that had started to fall in his terror.

Jimmy hung, covered in his own fluids. He had nothing left but broken hiccups of breath and screams that were making his voice hoarse. He didn't even remember the question that had been asked anymore as he felt the hand holding the small triangle of his skin began to slowly peel it away from his body. Then all he knew was pain.

Sometime later, he had no idea how long and didn't care. He heard that simple, quiet, and clear voice that gave him nightmares in life now speak a single sentence, "That's enough. I've learned what I can." He didn't so much as hear, but feel what happened next, when what sounded like a melon split open for just a fraction of a second and his world turned black.

***

Jimmy stood there, on the killing floor of his body, looking at what remained of himself. He looked pitiful, hanging there like that with his brains splattered all over his body. He was still hanging on the hook, but now, looking at himself, he understood the true scope of what they had done.

They'd literally peeled as much skin as they could from his body without killing him before just ending it with something exploding his brain. He stood vigil as the thugs took the bodies down from their hooks and tossed them into waiting bags for transport. Science wouldn't get much out of any of them.

As he was, Jimmy tried his best to process what had become of him. He knew he was dead. There wasn't a single question in that conclusion. He did have regrets, though. First, as they put him in a bag, he wondered if this was how they'd taken his brother away. If all he'd been was a body in a bag in the back of a car as it went wherever it needed to go to get dumped.

He thought of his own decisions following that event and now regretted waiting so long to move on Yensen. If they'd been there earlier, they wouldn't all be dead. If they'd gotten Yensen's money, they could all be living in some place nice in the middle of nowhere, enjoying peace and quiet. While there also wasn't any question of the peace and quiet of death, he'd have liked to experience it in life once. That opportunity was gone.

He thought of his two friends, Locke and Fence, and how he'd failed them so spectacularly. He'd known that Yensen had mob connections, but hadn't dreamed he was in as deep as he was. He thought about what would happen now as he watched himself and looked around. He'd expected Locke and Fence to be somewhere near him, as their bodies were also here, but that clearly hadn't happened. For the time being, he was all alone.

He watched silently as the bodies of himself and his friends were disposed of, and looked at the small strings that held him close to his body. The three of them were in a pile now, sitting like luggage in the corner while the men cleaned up after the grisly experience of killing them.

In the quiet silence, he noticed a small mist flow into the building, although none of the men did anything about it. Through the mist came a figure Jimmy had never seen before, and with it, he saw the shadows of his friends, standing much as he was. He called out to them as they did to him, but none could hear the others.

The figure that walked up to him looked like a bulky samurai from some kind of movie to Jimmy's eyes. It was cloaked and carried a sword. He looked closer and noticed that it was either very hairy or it was covered in fur. This fur was not well taken care of, and on closer inspection, this held true for every part of the being. When it looked at him silently, he looked into piercing yellow eyes.

Whatever this was, it didn't say anything as it stared hard at him. It stared for what felt like an eternity. Its hand slid back and forth from sword to sword on its hip, deciding which sword to pull free from its sheath. It surprised Jimmy to see two of them, as well as the indecision that the beast had regarding him.

Rather than take out either sword, Jimmy watched as what he could only describe as a bear took the thin strands that connected him with himself and tore them apart with his hands.

Chapter 7

Patches stood looking into the man before him and decided that he didn't want to deal with this. In rare cases, he would choose not to use either sword and instead rip the bindings of the soul from their bodies to allow them to make their own choice.

He grunted in annoyance. These souls rarely crossed his path, and in fact, he'd only seen three in his entire existence as a reaper of Elegy. It was her job, not his, after all, and he didn't want to make this choice. Too much work.

As the bonds tore and Jimmy's soul fled across the boundary between life and death, Patches stood stock still, looking inside. He'd felt another shift, but he didn't want to address it yet. He had a job to do first.

Sitting on the boat on the river Styx, Patches watched as the soul of Jimmy came back to itself. It was lying down in the boat, as many did, swaying in time with the rhythm of the small craft. He could almost read the face of the man as he processed what and where he was, as all souls did.

A surprising number of people had never heard of the river they were on, but almost everyone understood in some small part the necessity to cross from life into death. Patches rowed slowly while waiting for the man to figure it out. When he did, the man spoke, surprising Patches a little. Many people didn't say a word until they got to where they were going.

"Going to tell me what happens next?" Jimmy spoke slowly, and from his tone Patches understood it was nearly a rhetorical query. He did nothing but grunt in response, which, realistically, was all the answer the man needed. "I see you have a stunning vocabulary."

Even if Patches could speak, he probably wouldn't have said anything to the stupid comment it was. He could understand every language on Earth, although English was still his best language. He watched with some amusement as the man looked confused at himself sitting there, not used to his emotions being so... calm.

It was always entertaining when someone fully expected to lose a temper that they no longer had. Some emotion tended to cloud judgement that was necessary here, so part of his job was to take away some of the volatility and give it peace. He shook slightly in his amusement, his version of laughter in his afterlife.

He heard the man speak again, but he lost his ability to pay attention to him as his mind went back into himself. He looked again at his character sheet to see what had shifted inside of himself:

Name: Jimmy Stat

Titles: None

Race: Human

Class: Loan Shark

Level: 2

Current Experience: 300/400

Stat Points Available: 0

Strength: 12

Agility: 10

Constitution: 12

Wisdom: 17

Charisma: 15

Soul: N/A

Skills: None

To Patches' surprise, this man did actually gain his second level, although without being aware of the truth, his points were gained and distributed by deed, without his input. His actions gave all the necessary input, after all.

Patches looked again at the man, seeing if there was something he'd missed, but came up short. It was a hell of an achievement he'd gained, although he'd never know it. Patches himself was sure he was still a low level. It was just a guess, since he couldn't even read it.

All of that potential, wasted in death. He looked back to the river, having missed whatever his ward was going through as they passed quietly through the haze of existence that was the passage from life. He shook his head slowly, chewing on his stalk of grass, letting the taste permeate his boredom. He didn't care for the taste, but it had grown on him in the years, keeping him grounded.

He looked at his charge as they saw the docks in the distance, noting the wonder on the man's face. He was sure wonder hadn't been part of that man's life for a long time and was happy to give that feeling back to him, even if only for a moment.

He gave a final push as the boat neatly clicked in place, as it had for many years now, his strokes perfectly measured through the experience of decades. With the boat's arrival, he stepped up as he had hundreds of times, wrapping rope around the vessel so it wouldn't float away and waiting for Jimmy to join him.

He lifted a hand at the man, waiting patiently. It was important that each soul made their own way, although no one would ever tell them why. He just stood there, waiting, for the man to come along. Once

he did, he moved his hand to gesture forward, letting the man follow h
im.

Patches started down the path, making sure that they took each turn as required by the man's soul. He looked back every so often to make sure Jimmy was still following him. Seeing he was, he kept on the path. He watched as Jimmy's eyes took in the scenery as they walked, his wonder apparent. Patches himself didn't blame anyone for feeling awed at the sights. It was truly magnificent.

After the plaza, the two went through Jimmy's own personal pathway towards Elegy. They took twists, turns, a couple of truly enormous mountains and a few other things as they worked through Jimmy's life. They eventually came to the door that everyone reached; the carved stone double doors that led everyone to their last meal and their final judgement.

Much like every other, this soul's room was a banquet hall, filled with the food and drink that his soul would desire. Also, like nearly every other, at the head of the table, was his mistress, Elegy. She was different for everyone, and this time she was tall and slim, with pale blonde hair and a wide smile. Her skin was smooth as polished marble. Even while sitting, she was graceful.

Unlike many others, this room had two other people that Patches recognized as Locke and Fence from Jimmy's memory. They sat on one side of the table, and Patches watched Jimmy make his way over to them as he made his way to his mistress.

Behind her sat two others who worked for her, though he couldn't quite make out what they were. They were all both together in this room, and not.

"I'm sorry," was all Jimmy could say as he reached the other two. Patches thought he'd want to say more, but didn't have the words.

"If we didn't want to be there, we wouldn't have been," responded Locke. Jimmy nodded at him, then looked to Fence, taking a good hard look at her, not seeing any of the wounds he'd viewed her receiving.

Jimmy, quite dumbly, asked her, "You, ok?" The two looked at him and, unbelievably, began to laugh at him.

"You fucking idiot." Fence was laughing hard enough she had begun to cry, and she started to hit him. The first time it was a punch like one a friend would give to another's arm in companionship, but then another came, and another, and soon she was wailing on his chest. Her laughter had died as she hit him, and it soon reduced her to nothing but violence and tears.

After a period of a minute or so, it stopped abruptly, and she regained control of herself, no longer hitting his chest. "No, I'm not alright."

Having no way to respond to her actions, Jimmy looked to Locke and shared a look with the man, neither knowing what to do. After his look to Locke, Jimmy looked to Elegy, still sitting patiently, waiting for them. "Is this something you've done?" he asked, gesturing to Fence, who had completely regained control of herself.

"Yes, it is. Souls who suffer a lot in their last moments need help to cope with making decisions about their eternity," she answered smoothly, leaning back in her chair. "We can't have you making grave decisions about your afterlife just because you die horribly."

She continued speaking when the trio remained silent, "So on to the afterlife I just mentioned. Let's all take a seat and we'll talk about your options." She gestured at each of them to take their seats at the table. When they each sat, she spoke again. "First on my list is that I'm very glad you're all here together. I was hoping you'd die close enough to each other to allow it."

"I'm glad our deaths didn't inconvenience your plans for us," Locke said drily. His comment made Elegy laugh, and she held up a hand to allow herself the time to finish her laughter. The three watched silently as a single tear fell down her cheek in her mirth.

Elegy cleared her throat. "Delightful," she breathed as she got control of herself again. It expelled the impression that she could have been a mafia don from Jimmy's mind after that display. "You all can call me Elegy, and I'm the judge, although I don't judge so much as give you your options."

"And what are our options, then?" Jimmy asked.

"Your first set of options will be what you'll enjoy for your last meal," Elegy answered with a smile. "Everyone who comes gets one last meal before their decision. Just imagine what you'd like to eat and drink and it shall appear on your plate in front of you. It doesn't need to be anything on the table, it can be anything you like." She paused for a second before continuing, "I will wait until you all finish before discussing the next part of your options."

Patches watched as indecision clearly struck Jimmy at the idea of picking just one thing to eat. He both felt and watched the absolute torrent of ideas that went through his head over the course of just a few seconds.

Eventually, his mind settled on something... mundane, which surprised Patches. Or, more accurately, about seven mundane somethings. He ended up with a seven-course meal catered to his own personal tastes. Each plate was something simple, like medium-rare steak with sauce or even a small hamburger or grilled chicken with herbs. When he finished, then came the dessert he'd wished for.

His dessert was as interesting as his dinner, with a group of small dishes ranging from cake and ice cream to a turnover. Patches knew no matter how much he ate, he'd never get full, and that each bite he took would help him to feel a sense of closure and readiness for the next step.

When each was finished, they looked at each other, before all three of them turned to Elegy, who had sat in silence as the three gorged themselves on their last supper. With a smile Patches knew she had, she spoke to them again.

She tapped a finger on her chin as if pondering something and then looked to her guests again, "Now it's time for your other options, the bigger ones. It's time to think about your eternity. Like all of my guests, I give you your options for your afterlife," her voice hardened a little before she added, "As a warning, you won't get to discuss your choices together. Each person chooses their own eternity without interference.

"First option, you can go to be judged. Weigh your lives against the scale and see how you'll spend eternity. Second option, you can return to Earth; you'll be a ghost, only there to observe those you care to. Many lose their way on this path, but when you find your way back to me, you will *then* be judged and sent to your eternity.

"The last option... has not been taken by many, anymore," she looked up as she described the last option. "You have the option to go to a place to let loose your anger and frustration, where you can fight as long as you like. Like the second option, many can lose their way on that path."

The three sat quietly as she explained their options, and when Elegy finished speaking, Jimmy couldn't help but ask his question, "Which one did my brother Art choose?"

Elegy looked at him with a mixture of understanding, pity and sorrow before answering, "I can't tell you. It would alter your choice." She shook her head at him while shrugging her shoulders. "Sorry,"

Jimmy's face scrunched up as if he wanted to be angry, but the satisfaction from the meal and his previous unnatural calm seemed to prevent it. "Fine. How long do we have to decide?"

"As long as you need," her voice was kind as she looked at him, her face still showing some of her complicated feelings, "This place is here for you three and will remain as long as you deliberate."

Jimmy sat for a time, his reasoning beyond Patches and everyone around them faded to their own decisions as he began to speak. "I guess I'll take judgement. I'll see my brother again one day."

Elegy and Patches watched calmly as another soul passed beyond her realm.

Epilogue

E legy sat in her chair, staring at the surrounding baubles. In her natural state, something only other gods had ever seen, she was ethereal with eyes that constantly changed color, spanning the vast array of the rainbow and everything in between, much like a light whose color was never static.

Her body was as tall as a typical human's, at one hundred sixty-two centimeters in height, or five foot five for the Americans that Patches brought her. She'd always found them amusing, having to try to make things that were perfect as they were better for no reason.

She was slim, but not dainty, full in all the places that mattered to men. If she had an interest in romance, she'd have no trouble finding a partner. Elegy wore a black dress that suited her form, making her look like a pinup model, but again, it was all for her.

She sat looking at one of the artifacts in particular... one that had lain more or less dormant for over a thousand years. Where it had read the number one for all of those years, it had lit up with a new number. The number two, which told Elegy everything she needed to know about the truth of Tethir's return.

If she were lucky, it would read two and no more, but Elegy held no delusion of her own luck. If luck were feasible, then it would have remained at one forever. Another artifact sat next to the first, this one looking like an orb. It looked simple, like any gypsy crystal ball on Earth, but it held the power to look upon an agent of the divine.

She could use the orb to recall one she had sent to another plane, and did so now, recalling Shawn Wraine to her side. As he arrived, her form shifted to the one he had seen when he had died, as part of her essence was designed to make visitors at ease.

"What have you learned?" Elegy asked, already having a fair idea of the answer.

"It is as you feared...The world of Aardia has, indeed, come alive." Shawn spoke differently now than he had in his first life, and it likewise changed his appearance. She had installed him into a somewhat political role, the soul that had once inhabited the body lost in the transition. It would be hers once Aardia returned to her purview.

Shawn continued at her silence, doing as she had bidden him when he'd taken up his second life, "The world is in chaos, as rather than a true stoppage of life, the inhabitants were forced to live their roles for eternity, much like how a human video games' NPC might act upon Earth."

Elegy tilted her head to the side and down, looking at the floor as Shawn spoke, cursing the day Tethir had come into existence. "And what of the gods? Have they awakened?"

Shawn nodded his head a bit before continuing, "At this moment, I have detected only one god in the vicinity, although it is neither of the gods you are looking for. He too, has just awoken."

"Thank you, Shawn. You may return now. Good luck," Elegy said, using the orb to send him back to where he'd been before she called him. She had remained seated the whole time and now set the orb back on its shelf before letting out a heavy sigh.

If the gods were returning, then the universe would soon begin to move, and the only thing she could do was to try to prepare for it. She brought up a piece of information, letting it sit in her field of vision while she mentally scrolled through it as if it were a document or a web page on Earth.

In it were the names of every reaper she kept, along with all the information of their being. There were a few who would do if she needed to intervene.

Afterward

Niemara Helsar

It was all but literally a fucking circus. The police investigation, the court case, everything was one big damned carnival of idiocy. Niemara might have had a more elegant description, but decided it was wasted on these buffoons as she sat crossly tapping her fingers on the solid wooden desk she sat at. Her fingers tapped slowly, but picked up speed in time with her impatience at the process. Everyone knew how it was going to end at this point, but she was still required to sit through it.

Niemara had been going about her typical day, driving into town from her sprawling home in the outskirts of town to her law offices where she took on high profile clients who got into trouble that greasing the right palms could typically make go away. She was successful largely because she knew exactly whose palms to grease.

She strode into her office, her long legs easing up the space on the floor and looked at the mirror she passed each day that sat in the lobby, taking a moment to go over herself before stepping into the elevator. She looked as she always did. Niemara stood at roughly five-and-a-half feet tall with long blonde hair in a ponytail that went down her back that had long since begun to go grey.

With her lifestyle, that was the major indicator of her age. She didn't have many of the wrinkles set in that others in her age bracket in the mid-fifties held. Her skin was as smooth as porcelain, and her face was narrow. Her round eyes had brown that approached black in their cold and depth, and her mouth once had full and pouty lips, now thin from pressing them together for too many years.

She was modestly endowed, and could have passed for elegant on any day of the week. She was not, however, anything close to supermodel territory. As always, Niemara Helsar's primary demeanor was:

annoyed. Today, that annoyance was at being called in early on an emergency.

Her receptionist had taken a call from a new client who needed her as soon as possible. He'd been arrested the night before, caught by the police while transporting bodies to God knows where. She'd learned from her notes that his name was Marcus DiVino, and he had ties to a branch of the Italian mob. What they were doing in Ohio, she couldn't say, but it was now her job to represent a lost cause.

This wasn't the first time she'd been called on something like this, and she also knew it wouldn't be the last. Marcus himself was just important enough to matter, but not so important that he could make the seven police officers who had caught him disappear before testifying. So, as far as she was concerned, unless the D.A. fucked up, it was an easy paycheck.

That wasn't to say she wasn't waiting with bated breath for said fuck up to happen, she just didn't see it, knowing the man personally. He wouldn't miss a single thing she could exploit. Niemara had walked into the police station looking every bit as ice cold as she'd been accused of more than once before.

She knew the route to go to meet up with her client. He wasn't even being interrogated as the first thing he'd done after being read his Miranda warning, was to call for his lawyers. They'd taken one look at the situation and decided they didn't want the situation. They'd at least been kind enough to send their referral to her office, which had a 24/7 phone jockey for just such occasions.

She was led directly to his cell where she got her first look at her new client. One Marcus DiVino. She looked into the well-lit cell to find her new client sitting there with one leg crossed over the other and a small smile on his face. She'd seen similar smiles before, but she'd honestly never understood what it meant. It reminded her of a shark.

Ignoring it as she always did when encountering such an attitude, she looked at her client, "You called for a lawyer, Mr. DiVino?"